*This Book is **not** a work of fiction. My thanks go to my friend for unwittingly providing the framework for its contents and to my wife for consenting to be part of it all.*
The author, 2009

Six Days in Sicily – The Holiday with John

(A Viennese doctor invites his friends, an elderly Englishman and his wife, to spend a week with him in Sicily. This is the Englishman's account of their holiday together)

Herstellung und Verlag: BoD - Books on Demand, Norderstedt
ISBN 978 -3-8391-4844-0

1. John plans the holiday

John's suggestion came so unexpectedly – out of the blue – that both Doris and I were taken by surprise. We had gone out for a meal with him one day in April and were waiting to be served.

"What about a holiday in Sicily?" he said, looking at me, then at my wife.

"Sicily?" I said.

"The three of us."

Doris and I exchanged glances.

"How long for?"

"Only a week. I can't get away from the surgery for longer."

"And when would that be?"

"Soon. Before it gets too hot. You'd like it there. A friend of mine has just returned from a fortnight's stay. He was thrilled."

"But you've been to Sicily," Doris said. "You went with a Japanese girl."

"She was Chinese, and we went to Stromboli, not Sicily."

"Well, I know it was down there somewhere. You showed us photographs of the place."

Perhaps John realised that Doris and I were looking for a way to get out of going with him without hurting his feelings. We'd just got through a winter that had seemed never to want to end and were looking forward to watching nature re-awaken in the garden we have grown so fond of. To go off to Italy in the month of May would mean missing just that.

"We'll think about it," I said, meaning it, knowing how quickly a week can go by. John had so often wanted us to spend a holiday with him, but we had up to then always managed to wriggle out of his invitations.

"You wouldn't want to drive two old crocks around in Sicily." That was Doris.

"You're not old crocks."

"Born in 1928 and 1933 respectively," I put in. "We may not be crocks yet, but we're old."

I glanced again at Doris. She shrugged her shoulders.

"We'll think about it," I repeated.

"Do that. I can arrange everything through the internet."

We thought about it – long and hard. As I've said, we wanted to spend as much as possible of the dwindling time we still have left enjoying our wonderful garden. Apart from that, despite John's denial, we are old crocks, 30 years or more his senior. We are still pretty agile, but we also had the abrupt change of climate to consider and, like most people our age, are both on tablets for hypertension. I also have to cope with what medics, for want of a better word, term paroxysmal tachycardia, a condition in which, from time to time, when least convenient, the heart goes haywire. Our biggest concern, however, was John himself. He's a nice chap and we're very fond of him, but he's rather headstrong with a devil-may-care attitude to life. How would we three get on together. And then there was that other trait of his that called for careful consideration: his inability to be punctual. There's nothing, of course, abnormal in occasionally being late for some event or other, or in missing buses or trams, or even trains. That can happen to any of us and often does. But John misses aeroplanes; not just due to traffic jams in the city or holdups on the motorway. The fact of the matter is that John has made a habit of being late for everything, including plane departures, and I'm inclined to think it's because of the thrill he gets out of it. He's become addicted. He leaves everything till the last minute and then runs a race against time. Sometimes he wins and sometimes he doesn't. Repeating a phrase my mother often used when I was young, I've more than once said to Doris, referring to John, "That man'll be late for his own funeral."

It was a funeral, incidentally, that helped tip the scales in favour of our trip to Sicily. My brother passed away in mid-April, not long after our conversation, and I had to go to England to help lay him to rest. John thus had a further argument to work on; a holiday in Sicily would take me out of myself and put new life into me, he said, and both Doris and I had to admit that he was right. It wasn't that the event itself had been so strly nephew, Alan's son, had taken care of all the formaliti____d been what you could call a bystander. But laying a broth____s not something that increases one's zest for life. Add to tha____e of a journey to England and back and a week spent in a h____surroundings I knew so well and would, I realised, never again see had obviously taken their toll of my otherwise cheerful disposition. I was too thoughtful, John said. Perhaps I was still trying to figure out why my brother, a convinced atheist (when you're dead you're dead sort of thing), had expressed the wish – to me and in his will – that he wanted to be buried and not cremated. Atheists shouldn't worry about what happens to their bones after they've gone, should they? Well, he's now bedded down under a yew tree, a stone's throw from the west door of the village church, a prettier and quieter place than has been reserved for either me or Doris, who like to believe that there's a hereafter for all of us.

Anyway, at the beginning of May, the phone rang. It was John at the other end.

"It's me," he said. " I'm phoning to give you the dates of our holiday. We leave on May 13th and return on May 20th."

"May 13th? But it's my birthday on the 14th and Doris's on the 18th.

"Wonderful! We can celebrate both birthdays in Sicily."

"And it's Mother's Day on the 14th as well. What will our daughter think of that?"

"She'll probably be pleased about it. Anyway, it's all fixed. It's the hotel my friend stayed at. He was very satisfied. I've emailed the hotel. The rooms and the flight have been booked, both ways."

What could we do? We were faced with a fait accompli. We had condescended to go. We had only ourselves to blame. Then, slowly, it dawned on us how convenient the timing of the holiday actually was. Like many of our friends and acquaintances we seldom know what to give each other as sensible birthday presents. The week in Sicily would this year, for a change, solve the problem without more brain-racking. I would pay for the flight and Doris the hotel, or vice versa.

A few days before our intended departure John phoned again.
"We can't meet this evening."
"Why not? I asked.
"My mother's been taken ill."
"What do you mean?"
"She's been found unconscious on the bathroom floor. A neighbour alerted the police. We're waiting for the ambulance to take her to hospital."
"Okay. Keep us informed."
A mother found unconscious on a bathroom floor would have pulled the plug on anyone else's holiday but not on John's. As a doctor he was soon in full control of the situation. His mother, a widow, had lain there, it seems, for several hours, after slipping while climbing out of the bath, and wasn't yet quite herself. It hadn't been a heart attack or anything as serious as that. She was still in shock and it would take time, at least a fortnight in hospital, but she would be in the best of hands. And he wasn't an only child. He had a sister and a brother who could be relied upon to watch over their mother's progress and, via his mobile, keep him posted. We were somewhat less optimistic. What would happen if his mother died while we were in Sicily or, even worse, the day or night before we were due to leave? We were bound for Palermo, changing planes in Milan. That much we knew but no more. It occurred to us then how dependent on him we were making ourselves. Without him we would be more helpless than babes in the wood. The idea was rather troubling, but we didn't do anything about it. We hung fire and hoped for the best.
An important issue was keeping us awake at night and had to be discussed: how to get to and from Vienna airport. Should we go in John's car and park it at the airport for a week, or make use of the special taxi service Doris and I had often employed on our visits to England? As John had already pointed out, the difference in price was minimal, and it was much more convenient to travel in one's own car than rely on a taxi. But only ten days before, using his own car, he had missed a plane to Portugal and had been a day late getting to the conference there.

We opted for the taxi as the safer solution. Thank goodness we did! More about that later

"Both Doris and I think it would be better to take a taxi to the airport." He could see I was adamant about it. "We always do that," I added.

"Alright, I'll order a taxi and pick you up."

"No, you won't. The taxi will call for us and we will pick you up."

"Why that way round?"

"It's safer that way. We'll wake you with a phone call at 8 a.m. That'll give you plenty of time to be up and ready to go, assuming you've packed the night before."

2. We leave for Sicily

We ordered the taxi for 9:15 with the intention of being at John's place by 9:30. The night before, I rang him to inquire whether he had packed. He had! That put our minds at rest. We had stuffed (neatly folded) all our things into one conventional leather suitcase (thank goodness) and had only two small holdalls, so that, when the taxi arrived, ahead of time, we were soon inside it and on the way to John's flat. Such was his reputation, however, that I couldn't control the butterflies within me as we drove to pick him up. Would he be ready or wouldn't he? And what if his mother had suddenly taken a turn for the worse? Her condition had been stable enough over the last few days, but what if she had suddenly deteriorated and John had had to rush her to hospital? At 8 o'clock, when I phoned him, as arranged, there had still been no cause for worry, but in an hour and a half anything can happen when somebody has been found lying unconscious on a bathroom floor. I was, therefore, more than nervous as I rang the bell and spoke into the intercom. But, wonder of wonders, he was ready and would be with us in a few minutes! I breathed a sigh of relief. Things were going better than expected. Five minutes later he appeared at the door of the building and began to cross the street through the morning sunshine to the waiting taxi. But what was he was pulling along behind him?

A case big enough to hold a corpse! Why that size? We were only going to Sicily for a week! I didn't ask him what he had inside it. I guess I was too overjoyed to know that we'd get him to the airport in time. As mentioned, Doris and I were travelling light. If the boot had been just that little bit less spacious and our one conventional leather case just that little bit larger we'd have had to sit with it on our laps to the airport. Big, wheeled cases like John's are easy to pull but now and then they require lifting. However, my friend, though stocky, is a strong man and, with the taxi driver's help, got it into the boot easily enough. On the way back, when the taxi driver (a woman) and I had to handle it, she asked me whether my friend was transporting stones. But let's leave that till later.

We were amazed to hear that John had been up since 6 o'clock. He had actually been round to the hospital to see his mother and speak to the doctors there. Everything was under control. His mother was slowly becoming more aware of her surroundings and could be counted on not to have a relapse within the next week or so. That helped put our minds at rest. But our friend hadn't had time to inform his relatives – brother, sister, uncle – of the latest developments. Nor, for some reason or other, had he told them of his plans for their mother's/sister's future, that is, for the time when she would eventually be discharged from hospital. If she was to stay in her own flat it would need adapting to her new needs. John had it all worked out and, having greeted the driver, settled down next to him and took out his mobile. During the half-hour trip to the airport he spoke – non-stop – telling the family what would have to be done, as soon as possible, preferably during his absence, to ensure his mother could, in future, continue to live alone. It was obviously the first time the young taxi driver had had such a passenger beside him. During the journey, from my seat at the back, I could see how distressed he was becoming. At the airport he and I unloaded the boot – John still had the mobile to his ear – and, to help him over the experience, I explained to him that our friend was a doctor and that his mother had been taken to hospital.

The driver's laconic reply "I gathered that!" made me smile.
In the back Doris and I had been able to find distraction watching the landscape slide by, but the driver's right ear had been exposed to a half-hour phone call, and I thought he deserved a reward. I slipped him an extra-large tip. His face brightened. I often wonder how he described that drive to the airport to his friends before the memory of it faded beyond recall.

***

On the motorway we had been ushered once or twice by mounted police (on motorbikes) into the slow lane to facilitate the passage of some EU politician or other from a recent conference. We complied willingly, acknowledging, as it were, the right to priority of people responsible for Europe's future, whatever that will be. And anyway we were making good time. In fact it had taken us only twenty minutes or so to reach the airport and, after checking in, we had two hours to spare before take-off. John had never before had so much time on his hands before a plane departure and, having finally stowed his mobile, seemed not to know what to do with himself. Doris and I, on the other hand, were both relieved and pleased with ourselves. Everything was going so unbelievably smoothly. To cheer John up we suggested the snackbar, the one with a view of the runway. Our friend is having trouble with his weight. It's not that he's fat. As I have said, he's thick-set and muscular, but he's sensitive about it, which is understandable, for one could sometimes assume that he'd bought his clothes a size too small. He hadn't had time for breakfast that morning and was ready to tackle a pizza, provided we share it with him. My wife and I are not pizza fans, far from it, but, to please him, we accepted.
We were still busy with our pieces of pizza when John came up with it.

"We shall need a car in Sicily."

"To get to the hotel?" I asked innocently.

"Not only that. To drive around in. You want to see the island, don't you? This friend of mine has given me a list of the places worth seeing."

A few days before our departure John had already shown us the ten-page report his friend had drawn up for him, and we had wondered then how we could hope to cram everything he'd suggested into our six-day stay.

"So what do we do about it?" I said, never having rented a car abroad.

"Leave that to me. I'll contact a car rental agency at Palermo airport."

"How?"

"Through the internet. I can look for the cheapest offer, and it'll save time when we get there."

Not being internet fans we didn't quite know what he was getting at.

"I can do it now, from the airport."

"How long will it take?" I asked. We'd got him to the airport on time. I didn't want to lose him now.

"Half an hour."

Our plane left at 11:55. The time was now 10:30. We had almost an hour to spare before boarding. It sounded safe enough to let him go. He had his ticket and boarding card. He would meet us at gate 35. The idea did actually occur to me that what he now intended to do could have been done a week before or more, when he arranged everything else, but I didn't mention it. He'd been worried about his mother and it had obviously slipped his mind. He left us with the solemn promise to be at gate 35 on time.

***

Watching the planes take off I began to recall the last time Doris and I had sat in that same snackbar waiting to depart.

9

It had been the year before, in July, and we were bound for England, to spend our holidays there, unknown to us our last, in Bognor at my brother's place. We had more than an hour to spare and, like other passengers around us, had been whiling away the time over food and drink. The clock on the wall showed 11:45; departure was scheduled for 13:20, meaning that we would be boarding in an hour's time. My brother and a friend would be waiting for us at Heathrow.

We'd be there by 15:30 BST and through baggage reclaim by 4 o'clock. My brother's friend, an able driver, would get us to our destination on the south coast by half past five, unless, on the way down, as was our wont, we popped into a pub for a pint. That's how we'd done it for ten years or more – smoothly, without a hitch worth mentioning. This time it was to be different, quite different! We'd been in the snackbar for ten minutes or so, it seemed, when I happened to glance at the boarding indicator. Could it be true? Our departure to Heathrow postponed to 14:20 CET? It was true! The announcement of the delay was now coming through over the loudspeakers. Another hour had been added to the time we would have to wait. Ours wasn't the only flight showing the 'Delayed' sign, but that wasn't much of a consolation. However, as Doris pointed out, delays can be greatly reduced by faster flying speeds; we would simply have to grin and bear it. The two men meeting us would have to do the same. They were probably already on their way up to Heathrow and were now in a pub enjoying a refresher, the surprise of a longer wait for them still an hour or so ahead. Compared to what happened to the plane we were eventually to fly with a delayed departure is a bagatelle. Had any of the 200-odd passengers waiting for it known what was in store for them, they would probably have opted to wait even longer, for the next plane to Heathrow, which, in fact, got there before ours did.

We now had over two hours to kill, so, having finished whatever it was we were drinking we strolled off to inspect Vienna airport's shopping area, much enlarged of late. In the old days we could have wandered round the duty-free shop and bought fags for my brother and gin or whisky for his friend.

But, to many people's delight, in particular wellness freaks and teetotallers and, of course, above all, the EU states' finance ministers, an end has been put to all that. So we chose to browse in a bookshop among the paperbacks, most of them translations of bestsellers by American and British authors. Nowadays almost every American or British book you pick up abroad is or has been an international bestseller, some of them up to 300 pages thick.

How people find time to read books that length and yet attend sporting events or watch them and similar stultifying entertainment for hours on end on TV is beyond me.

Get interested in something, even if it's only leafing through books in a bookshop, and time, clearly a figment of the imagination, simply flies by. I must have spent half an hour or more in that bookshop but, more careful with money than in my youth, I left empty-handed. Doris had wandered off to the other section that sold chocolate and magazines (What a combination!) looking for something to read on the plane. My thoughts turned, as they always do when I enter a stationer's, to the millions of trees felled annually to produce the magazines and journals that fill the shelves. Not only that! Periodicals, replete with adverts, are not only growing in number, they are getting ever thicker! And those who produce them boast about it! How many, I wonder, end up half-read in the world's waste-bins?

A glance at my watch told me that we now had only half an hour to go till boarding, but the voice again sounding from the loudspeakers quickly put an end to that assumption. Departure had been delayed another two hours! To cut the beginning of a long story short, it was nearing seven o'clock CET when we heard that our machine was finally ready for take-off, having waited half an hour or more for a slot. At that moment our chief concern was for the two men awaiting us at Heathrow: by the time we got to London it would be around nine o'clock in the evening; they would have been waiting six hours and would be quite worried. Fortunately, like us, they didn't know what was still to transpire before we met, or they would have been even more worried.

According to the stewardess I questioned, the delay had been due to a late departure from Heathrow. That was not quite the truth. While sitting in the plane waiting to depart we got the whole story from the horse's mouth – the captain. At Heathrow he had been asked to pilot a plane with a defective undercarriage. Unable to steer the plane and mindful, rightly, of his passengers' safety, he had refused to fly it and demanded he be given a different one, which he eventually got.

Transferring the luggage and passengers to the 'new' plane and waiting for slots to leave Heathrow and land at Vienna had delayed the machine by four hours or so. He, the captain, acting, he said, in the best interests of the passengers, whose safety was at all times for him of paramount importance, asked for their forbearance and forgiveness for the long delay. We forgave him, knowing we were in good hands – which, to the misfortune of many now no longer with us, is not always the case – and would soon be airborne. The Vienna-to-London trip is more like a long bus ride. We expected to be at our destination within an hour or two.

During the flight the captain was very chatty and kept breaking the 'silence' with one remark or another, one of them a warning that there was thundery weather ahead and that the ride would be a little bumpy. He was right about that! More than once my heart popped up into my mouth, but the sight of the stewardesses going about their business, oblivious to the buffeting the plane was receiving, set my mind at ease.

The sun hadn't yet set over England and as we neared our destination its rays began to enter through the windows, first on one side, then on the other. That meant we were circling. We were used to that sort of thing, but we had begun to circle much earlier than usual. Before long the captain addressed us over the intercom. He was no longer so chatty. A severe thunderstorm over Heathrow was preventing planes from landing. With 16 planes ahead of us in the holding circle it would be half an hour before we had any hope of landing. But that wasn't all! We were almost out of fuel! The plane was in contact with air traffic control at Heathrow.

The captain had requested permission to take the plane down at Gatwick airport and was waiting for a reply......

Even as we approached Gatwick we could see the now darkening sky light up from time to time and knew that we had run into another storm or perhaps the same one, circling, as we had been. But storm or no storm, we had no more fuel! We thought of the planes that had crashed while attempting to land in driving rain because the captains had not been more concerned about their passengers' fate, and, given the choice, we would have preferred to stay in the air.

But we had to land. We held our breath and prayed. That must have helped. Or was it the captain's skill that saved us?

We landed at an airport that seemed to have closed down for the night. The ATC personnel were obviously still at their posts and had been waiting for the luckless BA machine we had chosen to fly on, but everyone else, it seemed, had either gone home or was sheltering from the torrential rain. We remained parked at Gatwick for half an hour, waiting for the storm to move on. With lightning around, we were told, there was no chance of refuelling. My guess was that the ground staff responsible for that job were being turfed out of bed, but I may have been wrong. No-one was allowed off the plane – for security reasons – so we sat there, glad to be back on terra firma but still praying. What then began to get me worried was the lack of fresh air: the front door of the plane had been opened but not the rear one. And why wasn't the air conditioning system switched on? Many of the passengers with larger lungs were chatting and laughing as if the whole thing were some huge joke, but others, including Doris, who suffers from asthma, were beginning to wheeze for lack of oxygen. I pushed my way to the front of the plane, where the crew were standing at the open door, now chatting as if nothing unusual had happened.

"There are people at the rear fighting for air," I said, butting in. "If you don't open the back door of the plane you're going to have a corpse or two on your hands."

It was the captain himself who answered. I recognized his voice. "The door can't be opened from inside. We're waiting for ground staff. They'll be here any minute now."

"What's wrong with the air conditioning system?"

"Out of order. Don't ask me why."

"I thought it was a new plane."

"So did I."

Thank God the captain was right about the ground staff! A few minutes later the rear door was opened, and we were asked to sit down to let the fresh air through. Another ten minutes and the storm had abated sufficiently for the plane to be refuelled.

Within half an hour we were on the way to Heathrow, skimming, it seemed, the trees and roofs of houses as we went. We reached our destination around midnight, eight or more hours late and well behind the plane that had followed ours out from Vienna. My brother and friend were still waiting. Kept in the dark about the incident, so as not to become too worried, they had planned to give us till midnight and then return to Bognor. The salt in the wound came when we went to pay the £34 parking fee. Doubtless, some of the passengers sued British Airways for what had happened. We didn't! Instead, on the way down south, we drank to the captain's health.

***

We didn't board through gate 35. Our gate number had been changed to 31 at the last moment. As was to be expected, John wasn't there, but the bus was waiting to take us to the plane and we boarded it – without John! It was my fault. I should have phoned him before, while we were on the way to the gate, but I don't often make use of my mobile, and it wasn't until we were in the bus, speeding towards the waiting plane, that I thought of it.

"Where the hell are you?" I said. "We're in the bus! And it's gate 31, not 35."

He must have been running when he got the call, for he was out of breath.

"I'm coming," he gasped and switched off.

Yes, but where was he coming to? Had he listened to what I'd said. I hoped to goodness he'd had time to consult the indicator. He's done a lot of flying and knows that gates tend to get changed capriciously. But even so, how was he to reach us in time without transport? It was a small plane. The bus we had stood in for ten minutes before leaving, obviously waiting for John, was the only one provided. He'd missed it! He couldn't run across the apron. That sort of thing only happens in films, and anyway it was too far and he didn't know which plane to make for.

In the meantime the bus had reached the small Al-Italia jet and the passengers were already queuing to mount the steps. Doris and I stood and looked at each other. I could see that she was sharing my thoughts. Was this going to be another missed-the-plane story? If John had been alone I couldn't have cared less whether he missed it or not. But he wasn't alone! He was taking us on a holiday to Sicily! And we didn't even know the name of the hotel he'd booked us into! And what about the return tickets? The paper for those was still in his possession. Why, having got him to an airport early for once in his life, had we let him go off like that? The future began to look very bleak.

The narrow steps up to the plane were delaying us and giving us more time to think. They couldn't leave without him if his luggage was on board. Or could they? Other planes had left without him. So why not this one?

Our worries came to an abrupt end.

"Sorry about that."

He was standing behind us, out of breath but smiling as if nothing of any consequence had happened. I flared up.

"What the hell happened and how did you get here?"

"That car brought me. VIP treatment."

We watched the car drive off.

"Why didn't you get to the gate on time?"

"I was trying for the cheapest offer. And it was the wrong gate number they gave us."

I didn't tell him he'd failed to consult the indicator. I was so relieved to see him that I didn't feel like saying anything more. I didn't even ask him if he'd managed to rent a car. There was something more important that had to be settled before we boarded the plane.

"Look," I said, "we have no idea where we're staying in Sicily. Where's the hotel and what's the name of it?"

"It's in Mondello."

"And where's that?" I asked.

"It's a suburb of Palermo."

Having said that, he produced a piece of paper, twice folded. It was the emailed confirmation of the booking from the hotel in Sicily. I took it and, without opening it, slipped it into my inside pocket and fastened the button. That would stay in my possession for the rest of the journey. Looking back that same evening, still in the car we rented, I felt like kicking myself for not opening that piece of folded paper, but if I had done so there wouldn't be so much to tell you about.

We climbed the steps to the plane.

"Buon giorno!" What a wonderful sound. So melodious. Much better than "Hello!" or even "Bonjour!". I love the Italians. It was love at first sight. Maybe I lived in Italy in a previous life. The train had stopped in Udine all those years ago and had filled up with happy people, complete with food and drink, which they proceeded to share with me. Hardly a word had been spoken until then, but when all those carefree talkative people climbed in, the compartment came alive. The Italians take life as it comes, seeming not to worry about the future. It must have something to do with the weather. Until now it may have been a good thing not to worry about the future.

Whether anyone, of any nationality, can afford to continue not worrying about the future is doubtful to say the least.

On entering the plane we were offered newspapers. I chose The Financial Times, which, in addition to business news, often contains interesting reading. John, I later noticed, as he sat on the other side of the aisle, had taken the Wallstreet Journal.

"Going into business?" I said jokingly.

"Not really. I've bought shares in one or two companies and I'm keeping an eye on them. It's so easy now to buy and sell through the internet."

So he was dabbling in stocks and shares, but how he would keep an eye on the world's stock exchanges while on holiday in Sicily was a mystery. It being a subject difficult to discuss across the aisle of a plane, I didn't pursue it further. I thought instead of all the people who, hungry for money, had gambled theirs away.

The refreshments on board were practically non-existent, but the flying time to Milan was less than an hour, so that didn't worry us. John didn't comment on it. Having downed half a pizza at Vienna airport, he probably wasn't hungry, despite the energy expended during his dash to the wrong gate.

***

The food served on short-haul flights has become absurdly meagre. Passengers were spoilt in the early days of air transport by copious meals, intended perhaps to take their minds off the hazards of flying. Better no food at all than what is nowadays offered you on short-haul flights, especially if you have false teeth that float around in your mouth.

The flight to Milan was over before we had time to get really settled in our seats. I tried not to think of the jagged mountain peaks below us. On the other hand, if a plane gives up the ghost at 10,000 metres it doesn't really matter what's below. You'll probably be dead before you reach it

Milan airport had us guessing for a while. The words "Uscita" (Exit) and "Transito" had been there for everyone to see but they hadn't seemed to be pointing anywhere. Thinking we'd missed an arrow somewhere, John forced his way back through the barrier to look again and was bawled out for doing so by a plump female official. Through her lips Italian didn't sound quite so enchanting. She didn't look Italian. Foreigners don't quite get the pronunciation right. But they have to be found work somewhere, so why not at airports? With his usual disregard for authority John ignored her and came back to us the way he had gone, upsetting the turnstile and probably breaking it. We didn't stop to check on that, but the plump lady's remarks followed us for quite some time as we made our way through the hall.

We had been warned what to expect at Milan airport. It was difficult, but we soon got the hang of it. You simply have to find the escalator and take it to the next level for inland flights. John had talked about a brief visit to the city but with only an hour or so to spare and my powers of dissuasion he decided against it and sauntered off to inspect his surroundings. We were now less worried about losing him. I had the email in my pocket with the name of the hotel on it and assumed that if he got lost and missed the plane he would know where he had chosen to spend the coming week with us. That assumption proved wrong, but let's take everything as it comes.

***

I still haven't figured out why the self-service snack bars in Italian airports are so organised: the cash-desk at the beginning of the array, the food spread out in the middle and the drinks at the end. That means you have to choose and memorize what you want before paying. As a foreigner with little knowledge of Italian you choose, then look at the cashier and gesticulate. However, given enough patience, on both sides, you can usually succeed in buying what your heart, or palate, is set upon.

Airport snackbars seem to be doing better nowadays thanks to the spartan short-haul on-board treatment one now receives, which would seem to confirm the adage about its being an ill wind that blows nobody any good. On the other hand, it could be the increasing popularity of food that accounts for the growing airport snackbar sales.

**

John soon joined us at the table where Doris and I were sitting, she munching the sandwich I had queued for and me drinking a glass of milk. Seeing us chewing made him want to do the same, and he went off to the snack-bar to buy himself something to eat. Before long he was back again clutching a huge tramezzino (Italian for sandwich) and attempted to foist some of it onto Doris and me. He often does that sort of thing: orders too much food, then remembers his wish to lose weight and tries to coax me or Doris to help him dispose of it. His problem is that he eats the wrong things. He doesn't care much for vegetables and eats very little fruit. He used to be a vegetarian, but under our influence has now (two years later) started eating meat – in very small quantities. What he lived on before I can't imagine, unless it was eggs, cheese and bread. Like Doris he's addicted to bread. To please him, Doris accepted a bite of his sandwich. I declined the offer.

**

Another thing I can't quite figure out is why people queue up to get on the plane hours before the boarding sign appears, when they could sit and read. Of course, many people don't like reading. Others, I suppose, want to get their hand luggage – often bulky – stowed in the overhead racks while there's still plenty of room. You could put that latter reason down to egotism, except for the fact that they also queue up to get off. They can't wait to get into the plane and they can't wait to get off it. It was the same in the old days disembarking from the Ostende-to-Dover ferry.

That was before the aeroplane came along. There was always such a rush for the gangplank you'd have thought a prize had been offered for the first person to leave the boat. You've probably noticed that people nowadays are always in such a hurry. They can't wait to get where they want to be and, thanks to the motor-car, often kill themselves trying to get there. Yet when they arrive – those that haven't killed themselves – all they do is waste their time watching some inane TV show or while it away pottering around in a garden, doing things that could have waited anyway.

***

There was a lot of heavy hand-luggage being taken aboard, so Doris and I thought it high time to join the now dwindling queue, or we'd be left holding ours on our laps. But not so John! He'd brought along a book and, after consuming that huge sandwich, had settled down to read. He sat there, within sight of the people queuing to board the plane, as if in a deck-chair on a pleasure steamer, seemingly oblivious to the sounds and sights around him. It could, of course, have been that he shared my opinion on the subject and was demonstrating his disdain. One of these days I'll ask him.

We were already in our seats and buckled up when he finally came down the aisle, the last person to board the plane. The stewardess was waiting for him. A married couple with two children, one still a baby, had been given seats in different rows. Her idea (the stewardess's) was that the four of them could sit together in the three seats across the aisle from where Doris and I were seated, provided John were prepared, of course, to accept a different seat. As he came nearer the stewardess addressed him. We didn't catch what she said, but to our dismay he refused – point-blank – to renounce his seat. Afterwards he said he hadn't liked the way they'd gone about it. He hadn't been 'asked' to take a different seat, he'd been 'ordered' to do so. When I reminded him later that the stewardess was Italian and the family French, he was prepared to believe that that could have explained their "lack of tact".

John showed no remorse but, although he didn't admit it, he probably regretted not taking the seat offered him. In the truest sense of the term the French lady had left her husband holding the baby, with the six-year-old boy to his right in the window seat and John to his left. From my window-seat on the other side of the aisle I glanced across from time to time. John, still on his pleasure steamer, was trying hard to read his book, and the Frenchman next to him was struggling to control the baby – both without much success. Like most toddlers the baby was restless and, bent on climbing, was finding its father's body of too limited scope. I expected John to explode but he didn't! He kept his cool throughout, seemingly ignoring the baby's attempts to use him as a learning aid to mountaineering.

We approached the island out of a cloudless sky. All I could see from my window seat was sand and I wondered how we were going to touch down on that. I needn't have worried. There was a splendid runway awaiting us, and a remarkably modern airport building with tinted glazing on each side of the air-conditioned corridors, through which it was a pleasure to walk. The luggage, we thought, could have come through a little faster; we were kept guessing for a while which carousel would deliver it up, but eventually, somewhere, a decision was reached and it began to emerge – with ours in first place! I let John handle his own luggage!

**

I didn't attempt to help John with his case for a very good reason. I had been in hospital once before through lifting a heavy case with a resultant rupture and didn't want to go through it all again. The weeks spent pushing that annoying little piece of intestine back into position will remain for ever in memory. So will the operation that kept me in hospital for six days or longer. I had been urged to have a coloscopy to check for cancer. More dead than alive after the senna-based purgative, I was filled with air till it came flowing out through mouth and nose.

As is often the case, insult was then added to injury: the day before the surgeon went to work on me I was exposed, naked from the waist down, to groups of young doctors, male and female, who were allowed to approach and palpate my abdomen. Fed on bread and soup for what seemed an eternity, I lost 5 kilos and was, understandably, craving for normal food again. I thought the male nurse was kidding when, after the operation, he told me there'd be nothing to eat till after the first solid stool. How on earth could I come up with any kind of stool after such treatment? "You'll see," he said, and he was right! He obviously knew more about that sort of thing than I did: within a few hours the stool was there! Where it had been hiding I'll never know.

3. John rents the car

So I let John handle the case later suspected (by the taxi driver) to contain stones, after which he strode off to the corner near the exit, where the three car rental agencies were located, side by side, leaving Doris and me to push the trolley. The two of us then sat down on one of the benches within sight of our friend and waited. The time was half past five. By half past six, we felt sure, we'd be at the hotel under a shower and by seven enjoying a good meal somewhere. Since breakfast we'd eaten nothing worth mentioning. My intake had been restricted more or less to a glass of milk at each of the two airports and the insipid coffee served on the planes.

***

Sitting in the snackbar at Milan airport I had looked around me at the many tourists, most of them stuffing themselves with food as if their lives depended on it. Of course, with too little food to eat life is a misery, but with too much of it available it's probably worse. As usual, there had been lots of obese people about, many of whom were carrying up to 30 kilos too much around with them.

When Doris and I go shopping at the weekend, usually on foot, she allows me to carry home the heavy carrier bags back from the supermarket, one in each hand, 10 kilos or so in all. I'm more than happy when I can finally dump them on the kitchen table. Many's the time I've remarked to Doris how strenuous it must be to carry 10 extra kilos around with you year in year out. She sighs, knowing what it's like carrying five kilos too much. But 10 is only a third of 30. Perhaps if your weight builds up slowly you don't really notice how difficult it has become to move from place to place. I must ask that nephew of ours if he can remember what it felt like when he began to tip the scales at 150 kilos and draw people's admiration as he walked by. They were no doubt admiring the fact that he was still able to walk. He slimmed down to 120 kilos a year ago and looked much the better for it. He'd been promoted to a new job, which involved flying to conferences in foreign countries. He hadn't flown for years and had forgotten what would be expected of him. He got inside the plane and down the aisle easily enough but then found himself faced with an embarrassing problem. Having squeezed himself into the seat, he couldn't get the two ends of the seat-belt to meet. The stewardess tried her hand at it but without success. Then after much discussion someone had the idea of lengthening the belt – by joining a kiddies' belt to it. The return journey was less problematic. With the outward flight still fresh in memory, my nephew was able to instruct the stewardesses how to proceed, but the experience had proved so traumatic that he decided to do something about it and, under his doctor's guidance, shed 30 kilos in 6 months, a feat of which he was very proud. Unfortunately for him he was demoted back to his former job and, no longer required to fly to conferences, has reverted to his 'normal' size.

One way of getting people to eat less would perhaps be to weigh them periodically and tax them on the amount of surplus fat they carry around. After all, it is well known that obese people are more susceptible to disease. Think only of diabetes, the treatment of which the thin ones among us, rapidly diminishing in number, have to help finance!

***

John had been at the agency counter for at least ten minutes and Doris and I were still waiting patiently on the bench. Half the people in Europe, it seemed, had descended upon Palermo that afternoon and were blocking our view. Slowly, however, they began to disperse and we were able to gain a better view of what was delaying him. Things were obviously not working out as smoothly as anticipated, despite the time spent "arranging it all" in Vienna. With his usual impatience over other people's incompetence he had got the teenage girl at the desk well and truly rattled. She sat behind the window, her arms held high, gesticulating wildly, and he, too, seemed to be nearing the end of his tether. It looked to me as if they were both having trouble making themselves understood. As we know, English is spoken everywhere but not with the degree of intelligibility required in certain situations, and, apparently, this was one of them. I was willing enough to help but didn't want to interfere. After all, the car was his baby. I approached quietly the scene of battle but remained some way off at the ready. From my position on his right flank I gathered that he had reserved a Fiat and the agency was trying to palm him off with a more robust but less nippy Mercedes. The girl had obviously not been at the job long and was no match for my friend, who was now attempting to draw the older person beside her, also of the fairer sex and attending to the needs of a second queue, into the fray. She, reluctantly, joined in but, even so, united, the two women were fighting a losing battle. It was clear that John didn't need me, so I withdrew and returned to my seat next to Doris. "It won't be long now." I said, but again my assumption proved wrong.

***

Watching the people slowly disappear through the exit into the sunshine I fell to musing about our situation. Why were Doris and I, two people in our seventies, waiting there like dummies to be taken to Mondello, when we could have been enjoying the peace and quiet of our garden?

For that matter, why had anybody else come to Sicily? What is it, I wondered, that prompts us Europeans to spend our holidays so far away from home? What are we looking for? Is it really a change of scenery or climate? Can't we find better ways of spending our, sometimes, well-earned leisure? Are we so bored with our own company that we can only get away from ourselves by flying to distant places? In our case, I must admit, we had come to Sicily first and foremost to please our friend, whose invitations to join him on his travels we had so often declined. But those others who had boarded the plane in Milan, people from all over Europe, from Germany, France, Austria, Holland and elsewhere. What had brought them here? Not a few of us even fly to countries on the other side of the world, sometimes never to return, victims of natural or man-made disasters too well documented to need enumeration. They used to say that travel broadens the mind, but few people travel nowadays for that reason. On holiday, today's tourists spend their time doing the sights, making the old-world cities of Europe look like outdoor museums; or they're out for relaxation, sunbathing, swimming, surfing, mostly uninterested in the country they have come to spend their holidays in and often leaving a trail of pollution behind them. Without the aeroplane this madness would not be possible, but like the motor-car the aeroplane is here to stay, despite its massive contribution towards poisoning the biosphere and depleting the world's oil resources. And we shall continue to fly to remote spots to get away from ourselves. And the world's airports and economies will continue to grow, rejoicing in the growing number of flights per day, because they mean bigger profits and, in most cases, the only way to balance the current account.

***

I looked across to the left. Why was John still at the counter? The girl was gesticulating again. We'd been sitting there for 20 minutes and there was still no sign of an understanding. What was the trouble now? I went over to the desk again.

They were discussing insurance: how much would it cost to cover an accident with possible injury or loss of life? €800 I heard the girl say. John had seen me approach and looked at me. I shook my head and grimaced, realising that fatal accidents can easily happen, but less often to careful drivers. In any case 800 was too much for my friend, who opted for a standard price of 180. With that the debate seemed to be nearing its end. All that remained to be done was for him to sign the contract and wait to be given the car-key. I retreated again to the bench to pacify Doris, who was sitting there, fretting. Who wouldn't have been? Half an hour to rent a car after all that time spent at the airport "arranging it all" before we left for Sicily!

Before the man eventually appeared, dangling a car key, John slipped into the nearby information office and came out carrying what turned out to be a map of the island. Things were now at last moving. We grabbed our luggage from the trolley. Doris and I were travelling light enough for short distances, but not for the route march ahead of us. I have never rented a car but if I did I would expect it to be a little less complicated. For ten minutes we stood at that airport exit door next to the man with the key, who kept looking expectantly westwards. He was waiting for somebody or something to arrive but what the dickens was it? It couldn't be the car, for he had the key in his hand. Most of the holidaymakers who had streamed out of the exit hall were milling there, still waiting for buses to take them wherever they were going. But we weren't catching a bus! We were renting a car! Why wasn't it standing nearby, waiting, ready for us to get into? Everything comes to him who waits. But when it comes you don't always realise it's there. I didn't! A mini-bus came along and people began to board it. I looked away for a moment, distracted no doubt by a pair of pretty legs (when it's hot some girls prefer dresses to jeans). When I turned back John, Doris and the man with the car-key had disappeared. I picked up the case and marched off past the bus to look for them.

"Where the hell have they gone?" I wondered. Then I heard Doris's voice.

"We're in the bus!" She was shouting from the door of it.

"In the bus?" I shouted back. "Why in the bus? We've rented a car."

"Get in and don't ask questions!"

She was pointing to a window seat. I looked and saw the man with the car-key. He had taken a front seat near the driver. John, behind him, was looking out of the window and beckoning. I heaved the case, now much heavier than before, and the larger holdall (Doris had the smaller of the two) into the bus and stood them up, wondering whether all the other people were also renting cars. Before I had time to put the question into angry words the bus had set off. I sat down and waited for the answer. It came soon enough. On the way to somewhere or other the bus was giving us a lift to the car-park. Within a few minutes we alighted to survey an immense compound filled with row upon row of cars glinting in the sunlight. The bus drove off and the man with the key began to thread his way westwards, John close on his heels. This was the route march! Picking one's way between tightly parked cars is tricky at all times. Carrying a heavy suitcase in one hand and a holdall in the other between cars parked bonnet to bonnet in double rows is a nightmare! We must have negotiated five double rows before our leader stopped at a blue Fiat Punto and opened it up to let out the scorching hot Sicilian air. Exhausted and bathed in sweat, I dumped my luggage and gazed, sweating profusely, at the car that was to carry us around for the next few days. To me it looked factory-new, but John didn't seem convinced, for he began to walk round it, inspecting it for dents. In case it only looked new, he didn't intend to be held liable for damage caused by someone else. Or was he getting his own back for having been led such a dance? Finally satisfied, he accepted the car, and the agent left us, wishing us a pleasant stay as he did so. We stowed our luggage in the boot and got in. For me, there was no doubt about it: the car was a new one. You could tell by the smell. That was probably why they had wanted John to take the Mercedes. They couldn't be expected to know that when my friend makes up his mind to something there's little anyone can do to make him change it.

***

27

The agency may have thought John not the right type to be offered a new car. I was tempted to think the same. Although over 40 and a doctor to boot, our friend is, as I've said, rather headstrong and creates a neck-or-nothing impression on people who don't know him. He even enjoys a brawl now and then. He called on us once, a year or so ago, with one eye blue and half closed and a gash in the side of his head, the result of some conflict he'd got himself into in a pub not far from his surgery. He seems to take more pleasure, though, in clashing with the authorities and, addicted to speeding, the one he most often finds himself up against is, of course, the police. He's had numerous tickets for exceeding speed limits and wrong parking and in many cases has gone into litigation over them, frequently coming off on top. I was once witness to one of his brushes with the Viennese peacekeepers. On our way from the city one evening he was signalled to pull up and into a side street by a young policeman not yet dry behind the ears, who asked to see his driving licence. John couldn't understand why he had been singled out for this purpose and began to arraign the poor chap for stopping him, a medical doctor, who was taking me, a professor of English, and also another Englishman, my brother, homewards, lawfully, in his car. The policeman, somewhat nonplussed by the berating, explained that it was a routine check-up and was being carried out throughout the city. Drivers were being stopped at random, not because of some offence, and he, the policeman, had, this time, by chance, picked on John. My friend was not satisfied with what he took to be an apology and began to lecture him on the rights of the citizen in a democratic country, pointing out that the police were there to protect them and not annoy them at every touch and turn for preferring to drive around in their own cars rather than make use of public transport, which was antiquated and unreliable. He thereupon demanded to know the policeman's number and name with the intent of reporting him to his superiors. Not wanting the two of them to come to blows, I got out of the car to mediate.

Placing a quieting hand on John's arm, I reminded him (in English) that he was talking to an officer of the law, however callow, and that the man was only doing his duty and had not stopped us because of some flaw in my friend's driving style or ability. To the policeman I explained (in German) that, despite all appearances, John was not a nut-case. He had obviously felt himself victimised and was all the more aggrieved because he had been taking me, a professor, and an English tourist, my brother, home. Under normal circumstances he would never have reacted in such a way. Whether the policeman really believed me or had got the wind up about being reported to his superiors I'll never know. In any case, without further ado, he gave John back his driving licence and, if I remember rightly, actually saluted as we drove away.

That happened two or three years ago. At the moment John is in a clinch with the London County Council. He was in England early this year and to get to his meeting in the North rented a car at Heathrow. Having a few days to spare before returning to Austria, he decided to spend the time in London – with dire results. On the day of his departure he left the car near Hyde Park, from where he phoned me – in Vienna – to say how wonderful it was to be sitting there basking in the spring sunshine. He had plenty of time, he said, to get to the airport but, as it turned out, not quite enough, for when he returned to collect the car it had vanished, towed away by London's traffic police. At the local police-station he was told why it had happened. The car, they said, having been illegally parked, had been removed to a better place. He could have it back on payment of £20. He must have been in a rare stew, for he had to fetch the car from the pound (the "better place" to which it had been removed) and hand it back to the rental agency, before boarding the plane for home. Of course, he missed the plane and forfeited his ticket. With so much money involved – the price of retrieving the car, plus £200 for a new ticket – he decided to take up the gauntlet.

Not long ago he received an answer to his complaint, giving him the right of appeal but, as I pointed out, with little hope of success, since the photos he took of the parking bay (to support his claim) clearly show that the space in question is for the use of local residents only. His chances of winning against the LCC are sadly remote.

***

I sat in the front of the car next to John, Doris in the back. My friend is an experienced driver and seemed immediately at home behind the wheel. We have been with him in his own car many times in Vienna and know how he likes to drive fast but we were not quite prepared for what was to follow. We left the airport at breakneck speed heading for Mondello. If anybody asks me today where Mondello is I can tell them exactly how to get there, but at that moment, as we raced hell-for-leather towards the motorway, I hadn't a clue where it lay and, as we were soon to discover, neither did John, except that it was on the outskirts of Palermo. I got the impression that he had decided to find the place by the trial-and-error method, but then I was suddenly reminded why he had slipped into the information buro. With his right hand – his left was on the wheel, thank goodness! – he thrust upon me a folded sheet of paper.

"What's this?"

"A road map of Sicily. Find Mondello and tell me how to get there."

"I thought you knew where it was!"

"I do, roughly. It's near Palermo."

He was still driving fast, too fast, and nearing a junction.

"Take it steady! You're driving too fast!"

But the junction was already behind us, and, by the sun, I could see we were heading south-west, away from Palermo."

"If Mondello is on the outskirts of Palermo, you're driving in the wrong direction.!

I had seen a signpost saying Trapani. We were driving away from Palermo, not towards it. Not believing me, he stopped the car at the side of the road and took the map from my hands. I was right.

At the junction he had turned right instead of left. Fortunately we had not yet reached the motorway and were on a sort of dual carriageway with breaks here and there in the row of oleander bushes that separated the two roadways. John assumed they were intended for U-turns and did one. Within minutes we were back at the junction.

"Slow down a bit," I said, "and let's look at the signposts."

But my advice came too late. We had already turned left and were racing back to the airport. We turned into the airport grounds. Back to square one! The second time round would be easier, I thought. We'd been that way before!

"If Mondello is on the outskirts of Palermo, let's go to Palermo and then start looking for it there. But for Heaven's sake drive more slowly. Then we'll see where we're going!"

John didn't reply but he did reduce the speed slightly and this time at the junction we turned left. I sighed with relief. We now seemed to moving in the right direction. John then spoke.

"What does 'Back to square one' mean?" He had heard me say it under my breath. I explained. He laughed.

"We've only lost a few minutes," he said by way of apology.

I looked at my watch. We'd wasted about 15 minutes but I said nothing. It was only 6 o'clock and the sun was still well above the horizon. Now that we were at last going in the right direction I thought we would soon be at our hotel. I have never been more wrong!

We turned into the motorway to join a double tailback of cars and came to a halt in the left-hand lane. A two-door saloon car came up close on our right. A pretty young blonde was at the wheel. John had seen her.

"She's from here. She'll know where Mondello is."

I let down my window. John leaned across.

"Scusi, Signora," he shouted. "Mondello?"

"Sinistra." she called back and waved her hand. We were moving again.

"What does 'sinistra' mean?"

I told him. John had been in Italy before and had picked up a few words of the language but, obviously, he had not yet mastered 'left' and 'right'. We needn't have bothered the woman, for a few minutes later we saw the signpost and turned off the motorway, destination Mondello. Things were not going so badly after all. Everyone makes mistakes, but when you're in a car and looking for the name of a street it's better to drive slowly. I mentioned that to John. He smiled and nodded, but the advice couldn't have sunk in deep. I noticed no change in his driving style.

So we were nearing Mondello, and I assumed this friend of John's had told him how to find the hotel. Slowly it began to dawn upon me that he hadn't.

"I thought you knew where to go," I said eventually.

"The hotel's in Mondello and we're not there yet. It's near the sea. When I see it, I'll know it's what we're looking for."

We continued, turning this way and that, each bend bringing us nearer the coast. Eventually I put my thoughts into words.

"The best thing to do would be to stop the car and ask somebody, preferably a policeman."

"Have you seen one?"

He was right. We hadn't seen a policeman since we'd been on the island, not even at the airport.

"Sicily seems to manage without policemen," I said. "Or perhaps they're on strike."

"Or chasing the mafia."

"What is Mondello anyway?" I asked.

"A holiday resort. It has one of the best beaches along the northern coast of the island."

"Then let's get nearer the sea. What's the name of the hotel?"

"Trabia, Hotel Trabia."

"Then instead of driving around in circles stop the flaming car and ask somebody where Hotel Trabia is!"

"Who's driving around in circles?!"

"You are! This is the second time we've come this way. I remember those wrought iron gates."

John didn't know what wrought iron was, so while he continued to drive, at a loss, it seemed, sometimes which turning to take, I explained the term. We still weren't getting anywhere.

"For Christ's sake stop and ask somebody!" I said, exasperated.

This time I must have got through to him, for he stopped. He had seen a white-haired man, standing behind a fruit stall, obviously the owner.

"He should know where the place is. Let's ask him."

The man was on the far side of the car. Lowering the window John called out.

"Scusi, Signore, Trabia. Hotel Trabia."

The man came across the street, and John repeated the question.

"Hotel Trabia? Trabia?" the man said, scratching his head hard for a while. He had obviously never heard of it. Raising his hands in despair (or was he apologizing), he returned to selling his fruit.

"If it's a new place an old man like that wouldn't know where it is. We must find someone younger."

(Actually, as we later discovered, we were very near the beach and the man would certainly have known the hotel had it been there.)

John agreed to my suggestion. We turned into the next street and found two young men about to mount their motorbikes. They looked more promising and would probably understand English. Again they were on John's side of the car He lowered his window again.

"Scusi, Signore. We're looking for Hotel Trabia."

"Trabia? Here no Trabia. This is Mondello. Trabia in province."

"There must be a Hotel Trabia in Mondello." Turning to me, "Give me the email you've got in your pocket."

I took out the folded piece of paper I had kept securely hidden away throughout the flight and handed it to John. We should have thought of that before. The name of the street was sure to be on it, and a street is easier to find than a hotel. Before passing the email to John I unfolded it and caught a glimpse of the heading. It read: 'Hotel Tonnara Trabia'. The man with the bike took the paper, looked at it for a few seconds, then spoke.

"Address says Trabia. Look."

Through the open window he showed John the address in small print at the bottom of the paper.

"But where is Trabia?"

"Province." came the reply and with a wave of the hand, "Cefalu, Messina."

There was no arguing. The address was Trabia. We thanked the man and drove on.

"Why the hell have we come to Mondello when the hotel is in Trabia?"

"We talked all the time about Mondello."

"Who did?"

"The chap who recommended the place."

"So you emailed the hotel and didn't look at the address?"

"Why didn't you look?"

"Because I assumed you knew where we were going! If you book rooms in a hotel you usually check which town it's in!"

It was at this point that Doris, who had sat through it all very patiently until then, probably asleep most of the time, chimed in.

"Arguing won't get us anywhere. Look at the map and see where Trabia is."

That was one of the excellent suggestions Doris occasionally comes up with. I took the map and studied it for a moment. I found Cefalu easily enough and a place called Bagheria nearer to Palermo, both of them on the coastal road leading eastwards. But it took me a good deal longer to find Trabia. If the print had been any smaller I'd have needed a magnifying glass.

"I've got it! It can't be much of a resort. The print's so small it's hardly legible."

I expected John to stop the car and consider how to get there, but he didn't. He continued driving and told me to guide him.

"We're on the west side of Palermo," I said "and Trabia's to the east. To get there we'll have to drive through the whole of the city and then head for Bagheria."

That would have been as easily done as said, if we'd had a large-scale map of Palermo but we hadn't!

We found what seemed to be a main road leading eastwards through the city's coastal district and took it, but everyone else in the city was obviously intent on going that way, too. In the old days the Italians used to go strolling in the cool evening air. Nowadays they seem to take to their cars. I have driven in many cities at peak hours in my own car and I've been in no end of traffic jams but what happened that evening on the way to Trabia defies all description. Istanbul, the worst city for traffic I'd been in till then, pales in comparison. We couldn't have picked a worse day or time than Saturday, May 13th, eight o'clock. Where were all the people going? Were they really just driving around or had they all some destination in mind? There were cars everywhere, of every shape, size and age. However, although the street was jam-packed, we were moving – a metre at a time – and from the side-streets cars kept coming in to join us, hooting as they did so. Could it be they all had defective brakes, or perhaps no brakes at all? John forced his way forward, competing with the other road-users in driving style and hooter use. How he avoided hitting anyone that day I'll never know.

***

Talking about hooter use, how many of us commit minor driving errors from time to time and are aware of it. Do we need to be reprimanded by the blare of someone else's hooter? I have noticed that over the years car drivers everywhere have become increasingly undisciplined and egoistic. Of course, the number of road users is constantly growing, which makes for greater friction, and the need for self-restraint is learnt these days neither at home nor at school. The love-thy-neighbour behaviour preached when I was young has, it seems, gone out of fashion, like Christianity itself, which promoted that and other ideas, many of them too far out for serious consideration. Psychologists assert that at the wheel of a car the motorist displays his/her true character, and yet what a wonderful opportunity driving offers us to be chivalrous.

Could this, I wonder, one day help outweigh the many negative aspects of the motor car, one of them being that since its invention 10 million people have died in their cars on the world's roads? Not to mention the many more millions dead and dying from traffic-related diseases.

***

Driving through Palermo on that Saturday evening was a nightmare. If once, I must have said "Watch it!" a hundred times. An accident in a foreign country in a rented car was the last thing either Doris or I wished for, but John didn't seem in the least concerned.

"Where are they all going?"

"Your guess is as good as mine," I replied. "They can't be going home from work. It's Saturday."

"Maybe they've come from a football match."

"Or are going to one. Watch it! You nearly hit that blue car."

"A miss is as good as a mile."

"Correct, but there's no need to drive like a maniac."

"When in Rome do as Rome does."

"We're not in Rome, we're in Palermo, which is probably worse."

"I've never driven in Rome."

"Watch that one coming from the right."

"Leave the driving to me and tell me how to get to Trabia."

"Bagheria's ahead. And Bagheria is about half-way to Trabia. And next time we go on holiday together, if ever we do, make sure first which town the hotel is in!"

"We're never going to hear the last of this."

"Right again."

I must admit he was handling the car as if he'd been driving it all his life. He was beating the Sicilians at their own game. I suspected he had driven such a Fiat before. But it was getting late and though we were moving faster now, it would be turned nine o'clock before we reached the hotel.

"What do we do if they've assumed we're not coming and have given our rooms to someone else?"

"They can't do that."

"Why not. We're two hours late already. At this rate, by the time we get there it'll be near midnight. I think we should let them know that we're coming."

Doris agreed with me. "There's no need to tell them we went to the wrong town. Tell them we stopped in Palermo for a snack."

"Okay, I'll phone the hotel and say we're on the way."

John picked up his mobile.

"And that they should keep the rooms you reserved – facing the sea."

"Read out the number. It's on the email."

I read it out to him and John spoke to the hotel reception. The rooms were still waiting for us. That was a consolation, but, by the look of it, we still had a long drive ahead of us.

The word 'snack' had roused Doris's appetite. "Why don't we really stop for a bite to eat somewhere."

"What a wonderful idea!" John said.

"No," I said, "no stopping for food or we'll never get there."

I had my way. We didn't stop. A few minutes later John had an even better idea, one that should have occurred to him, or me, earlier, much earlier.

"Let's get back to the motorway."

"Why didn't we think of that before?"

"Keep your eyes peeled for a signpost."

"Alright, but drive a bit slower."

We had left the dense traffic and our friend was getting into his stride again. Some minutes later I saw a junction ahead with a road branching off to the south, away from the coast.

"Autostrada. Slow down."

He reacted quickly and we turned onto a road that promised to take us eventually to the motorway. We'd be there sooner than we'd thought.

"The rooms are air-conditioned?"

"Bound to be."

"Your friend confirmed it?"

"He couldn't remember. They were there in autumn and didn't need air conditioning."

"I hope we're not going to get bitten to death by mosquitoes."

"There aren't any mosquitoes near the sea."

"You must be joking." I said, remembering the week spent in Grado some years before.

***

If there's anything I dislike it's being preyed on by mosquitoes. They are bad enough in the daytime when you can defend yourself with a slap here and a slap there, but at night, in the dark, you lie in bed at their mercy. They come and feed on you! You can soak yourself from head to foot with repellent but, ten to one, they'll find a spot you've overlooked.

I'm not the only person who dislikes mosquitoes, witness the many black splotches you find on hotel room walls, too small to be the remains of squashed flies. Who hasn't woken up in the middle of the night and heard that high-pitched whine? You don't put the light on because you're a considerate person and don't want to wake your partner. So you slide down under the quilt, or sheet, or whatever it is you're under, leaving only your head and a hand exposed, and wait for the enemy to attack. Where she lands (as we all know, it's a she not a he) can be roughly gauged, and you whack the spot hard with the palm of your hand, following it up with a circular rubbing motion, to make sure the enemy has been totally obliterated. If the whine comes again you misgauged her position, or she was not alone. Repeat the operation or give up and go into permanent cover, face and all.

4. We find the hotel

We reached the motorway again at 8:20, having left it at around 6 o'clock for Mondello, and reached our destination at 9:15, a record time of three hours to cover 60 kilometres. It would have been almost as quick on foot – without luggage, that is. The journey from the airport would actually have taken us 40 minutes at John's motorway driving speed but, after all, we'd had the pleasure of passing through Mondello, albeit without seeing "one of the best beaches on the northern coast of Sicily".

We had left Bagheria far away on our left, and I had thanked God we weren't still labouring along the coastal road, which would have prolonged the journey by another hour at least. When the name Trabia finally showed up in the beam of the headlights Doris and I sighed with relief. Even John, who was now in his element, enjoying himself at the wheel, seemed pleased our odyssey was soon to end. The speed bug had him in its grip, and he was driving too fast for our liking, but we said nothing, knowing how eager he, like us, was to get to our destination. He approached the exit road at such speed that, for a moment, I thought he had decided to carry on along the motorway and look for a hotel somewhere else, in Cefalu perhaps. At the last moment, however, he jammed the brakes on, taking us from the motorway at 80 kph, but speeding up again on reaching the highway. It would be child's play, we agreed, to find the hotel in a small place like Trabia. The road was running quite close to the shore. The village or whatever it was would be on the right side, and he was preparing to turn off, still travelling fast.

"Slow down, for Christ's sake!" I said. "How can you expect to find anything driving at this speed?"

"And if the hotel is on the shore why are we driving away from it?"

Doris's remark sank in, and John slowed down. It was at that moment that we spotted our Eldorado. But was that it? It looked more like something the Knights Templar had left behind, or was it the Vikings? It was a fortress-like edifice, some hundred metres in length and strung out between highroad and beach.

But from the car, now stationary, we read the name clearly marked beneath the crenallation 'Hotel Tonnara Trabia'. This was certainly the place we had been looking for for the last three hours! And Doris had saved us from a vain attempt to track it down in the village. I could have kissed her for that, and probably did – later. John turned the car and we drove into the small car park to the right of the building. Destination reached at last!

Within minutes we'd be in our room overlooking the sea, me under the shower and Doris unpacking. At the reception desk we collected our keys – for rooms -228 and -229, two floors down. No one offered to show us the way. Why should they at that time of night? John had begun to chat up the girl receptionist, so Doris and I left him improving his Italian on her, squeezed ourselves with our luggage into the small lift, pressed the -2 button and descended to look for our room, hopefully not underground? Like the hotel itself the room was to prove hard to find. Bewildered by the unusual layout of the place, we took a wrong turning and found ourselves in what resembled a medieval courtyard, where a very self-assured blonde lady was lecturing a group of smartly dressed guests on the history of the hotel. Scattered leisurely around her, they seemed more interested in what they were drinking than the guide's discourse but they were enjoying themselves (in the cool evening air), and that is what holidays are supposed to be all about. Standing there, suitcase in hand, hungry and still sweating from our peregrinations, I felt rather envious of these people. If we hadn't spent so much time in Mondello, looking for a hotel that wasn't there, we could have been among them, sipping champagne and listening to the guide. We would have found it hard to follow, for she was explaining things in Italian. English or German would have been a different matter, but then again would it have been presented in a way to grab our interest? At work many people are square pegs in round holes, and tourist guides are no exception.

At that moment John joined us, pulling his big black case behind him. He is a clever man, but he, too, was finding it difficult to locate his room.

Our only consolation was that from where we were standing we had a clear view of the sea. We were not going to sleep underground after all. We'd got the floor right and that was on seashore level! I was just about to carry on about the lack of organisation, thought to be typical of the country we were in, when a pretty though portly lady, elegantly dressed in a black costume, appeared from nowhere to rescue us. Seeing us standing there like lost sheep, she had apparently been filled with compassion. She beckoned us to follow her and led us through a maze of corridors to our rooms. Whichever direction we had taken on stepping out of the lift, we wouldn't have found them, not in a month of Sundays. Later when we got to know the lay of the land it was child's play, such is the capacity of the human brain, even at the age Doris and I have so quickly reached. As I pushed the key into the lock I turned and said, "Grazie." The lady in black simply smiled and walked away.

***

I later began to wonder who our guide in black had been. Was she the owner of the place or only the manageress? We met her in the corridors once or twice during our stay and each time she was wearing the same elegant black costume. Now I come to think of it she never spoke but only smiled at us and nodded. If I were of a more imaginative turn of mind I could perhaps kid myself she was not quite real. Not that I don't believe in ghosts. I do. I've read many a ghost story. Not silly ones thought up merely to make money in the form of books or, worse still, films, which, too far-fetched to believe or badly written or directed, only serve to ridicule the phenomenon and increase the number of non-believers.

I myself have never seen a ghost, but I once knew a man who had. He's been on the other side for many years now. He was a Latin professor at the school where I used to teach. He was also a healer. As a youth he opted for a monastic school with the object of later taking holy orders. The chapel adjoining the school was said to be haunted by the figure of a monk and whoever saw the apparition hadn't much longer to live.

One afternoon he and two other lads were in the organ-loft when they saw a figure in monk's clothing slowly cross the chancel and kneel down in prayer before the altar. As they watched, so he said, the figure slowly melted away and left them wondering whether they really had seen the figure or imagined it. They were laughed at when they told the other boys of their experience, but within a month his two friends were dead; one was killed in a road accident, the other died of blood poisoning. He himself lay at death's door for several days with double pneumonia. As I said, he was a healer. Perhaps he was allowed to live in order to help others. In any case he didn't become a monk!

***

We arranged to meet John later in the restaurant and entered the antechamber of our appartment. Through the half-open door we could see that the bathroom was not the last word in luxury, but that didn't worry us. Taps and bathroom fittings needn't be in gold, neither for me, nor for Doris. The main thing is that they work and, as we later discovered, these did their job admirably. We then entered the bedroom that was to be our abode for the next six days. We were impressed. Spacious and lofty, it was nicely furnished with wardrobe, desk, studio couch, TV set and, for Doris and me (two oldeys) the most important piece, a large double-bed, neatly made up and covered with a fine hand-embroidered counterpane. The most striking object, however, were the curtains that ran the full length of the far side of the room, which, I thought, must surely face the sea. I placed the suitcase on the stand provided and walked across to inspect them. I was most impressed. At some hotels they seem to think you are used to rising with the lark (Are there any larks left?) and hang see-through side curtains that, more often than not, can't be made to meet in the middle, or simply make do with lace curtains. Of course, the intent of hotel owners could be to get you out of bed early and down to breakfast quickly, so that the chamber maids can perform their daily chores promptly and return, without the need for overtime, to their dogs and cats – or hubbies and children, if they have any.

The curtains in this room were the finest hotel curtains I have ever seen! They were of brocade, heavy and luxurious and lined to keep out the morning sunlight. I drew them back to reveal a large shuttered French window, which I opened, shutters and all. I couldn't believe my eyes. The sea was less than a stone's throw away. We were on a level with, and separated from it by, what looked in the dark like a wide strip of lawn. On all my seaside holidays I had never been in a room like that! We were, at the most, 10 yards from the sea. I could hear the waves lapping on the beach and saw already in my mind's eye the room as it would be the next morning with the daylight streaming in through the window. The journey had been a nightmare, but our stay at the hotel was promising to be exactly the opposite.

We had booked into the hotel for bed and breakfast only, but it was getting late, so we decided to have our first evening meal there. We took the lift up to the restaurant, a large elegantly furnished room with small lamp-lit tables neatly arranged around a central buffet. As we walked past this to a corner table I noted, my mouth watering, the dishes full of tasty Italian hors d'oeuvres and felt sure we had come to the right place, if only to enjoy such delicacies. A dapper waiter brought us the menu. Eight euros for the antipasto was not what you'd call cheap, but what you fancied to whet your appetite seemed limited only by the size of the plate. John kept his going with a second plateful, secured while the waiter was busy elsewhere and eschewed a main course. Doris and I opted for some moderately expensive pasta-based dish or other, the name of which escapes my memory. We finished with a bottle of white Sicilian wine and were impressed enough to make a mental note of it for future meals there or elsewhere on the island.

The 'drive' from the airport had knocked the stuffing out of all three of us, so we paid the bill and turned in, in agreement that the hotel could be explored more effectively in daylight.

It was nearly midnight, and Doris and I were already stretched out in bed, reliving the events of the day and thanking God that we were at our destination, when we were roused by a light knock at the door. I answered it. John was standing there in his pyjamas.

"What's the trouble?" I asked.

"Can you hear that noise?"

I listened.

"Come out into the corridor."

I obeyed and listened again. Straining my ears, I could just discern a faint throbbing sound as made by a diesel engine.

"It sounds a bit like a motor, but it's not all that loud."

"I thought only Doris was deaf!"

I must admit, like that of most people my age, my hearing is no longer as acute as it used to be. It's the high frequencies I no longer hear so well. When John's mobile rings, for instance, I never hear it. Once or twice, before I cottoned on, I used to wonder what made him jump up from his chair, as if stung by a wasp, and go rummaging in the briefcase he would leave in the hall when visiting us. To a person whose sense of hearing was so keen it was clear that this noise could prove disturbing.

"What do you think it is?" I asked, although I knew the answer. On first entering our rooms and again on retiring I had noticed that we were very close to the hotel's indoor swimming pool, visible through a glass door. John had been given the room next to it.

"It's pretty obvious what it is! It's a pump for the pool. To keep the water circulating."

"All night long?"

"It hasn't stopped since we came back from our meal."

"Get them to switch it off."

"I've phoned reception. The chap in charge has gone off to bed. And anyway it has to stay on."

"So what are you going to do?"

"One thing's for sure. I can't sleep with that thing going all night."

"We've got a studio couch in our room."

But he was already examining a box set flush in the wall opposite his door.

"What are you doing?"

"If I'm not mistaken this is a fuse box."

"You can't switch the pump off from there."

"No, but I can remove a fuse or two."

And he did! We said goodnight to each other and hoped for the best. There were no repercussions.

5. Our first breakfast

At six o'clock I awoke to daylight. Before going to bed, despite the tiny blotches of dried blood on the walls (left behind, of course, by squashed mosquitoes) I had opened the shutters and drawn the curtains back wide to let the sea air in while we slept. I tiptoed to the window and looked out. What a wonderful scene lay before me. The French windows opened onto a narrow bridge accessing a strip of lush grass and a narrow beach of pebbles. Beyond that a few tiny fishing-boats were bobbing, at anchor on the water of a small bay. Further out, forming a breakwater, stretched a long stone jetty and, still cloaked in mist, lay the open sea, the Mediterranean! Back in bed with the curtains drawn close, I was soon asleep again, lulled by the prospect of a pleasant week in Sicily. We probably had one of the best rooms in the hotel! John had the worst. Once again my horoscope was proving true: lucky when on holiday.

***

Breakfast was from seven to ten. We had arranged to meet John at nine thirty in the breakfast room, but after a day spent on the road and with those thick curtains turning day into night it was foreseeable that we wouldn't make it. It was, in fact, nine thirty turned when I re-awoke and with a kiss drew Doris gently back to reality. Within minutes we were washed (a catlick) and dressed and on our way, at the double, to the breakfast-room

More haste does result in less speed, especially in a strange hotel! After spending five minutes or more rushing round wrong corners we finally discovered the lift that had brought us down to the -2 level. With a "Buon giorno" and a wave of the hand the pretty girl at the reception desk pointed to a second lift, destination breakfast-room, which we reached about 9:45. John was there trying to organise food and drink. For some reason the breakfast staff had not been informed of our presence at the hotel, nor of our desire for food, and had already cleared the decks of everything eatable. Had we stayed at home I would have been at that moment, as every year, tucking into a special birthday breakfast. Instead, I was faced with the prospect of having to make do with warmed-up coffee and whatever food had been left over by the early risers. However, things turned out somewhat better than expected. At John's behest the waiters, straining to pack up and leave, reluctantly carried back the salami and cheese, and the three of us sat down to a frugal makeshift meal. We weren't all that surprised about the simple fare. From previous holidays we knew that, like most continental Europeans, the Italians prefer to go to work on a half-empty stomach. And we weren't alone in that huge sunlit room! Searching for something to eat at an empty buffet table I had turned to a girl in white to my right and asked, in English, where the dickens the food was. Indignant, she had replied (also in English) that she didn't know, because she wasn't a waitress but a guest at the hotel, like me hungry and looking for food! She and her husband eventually sat down at the table next to ours. They were from Holland and had come from the airport by train. What a sensible thing to do I thought.

***

Sitting, on my birthday, in that over-large breakfast room, forcing down a salami sandwich with the help of warmed-up coffee, I fell to thinking of England and the magnificent breakfasts I had eaten there in its hotels and boarding-houses. What a difference to what I was now chewing.

Eat a well-cooked English breakfast and you feel good for hours! If I remember rightly, Somerset Maugham praised the English breakfast as a wonderful invention that should be eaten three times a day? Having lived on the Continent for 50 years, I would second his praise but not the recommendation. Not because I consider it a major cause of obesity, as some nutritionists would now have us believe, but because anything eaten too often, even caviar, tends to pall. And although the English breakfast can be varied to an extent undreamt of by those born outside England, three times a day could prove a little too often. While on the subject of food, perhaps you'd like to know that there's a joke circulating in Austria (told to me by John of all people), in the form of a question as to which is the smallest book in the world, the answer being an English cookery book. In defence of English cooking I referred him to Mrs. Beaton and co. and described the scrumptious meals I was brought up on in Yorkshire and those Doris and I were regaled with when on holiday at my parents' place in London.

As a teacher I was often asked by pupils back from holidays in England why food served there in restaurants was so bad. I replied that food at non-English restaurants is also very often not worth writing home about, the reason being that restaurants everywhere are profit-making concerns created to procure for their owners the highest returns for the lowest investment. The employment of good and dedicated cooks, who, by the way, like good artists, are few and far between, would for most restaurant proprietors result in low profits.

And yet, despite the decline in quality (and amount) of the food served at the average restaurant, more people seem to be eating out nowadays than ever before. Are women (and men) losing interest in cooking their own food? Is cooking going the same way as sport? Do people prefer to watch rather than practise it. If so, that would explain the innumerable TV shows devoted to cooking and the many coffee-table cookery books nowadays on sale, replete with seductive photos.

Could it be that women in our industrialised world, spoilt by the wide range of fast foods now available, are losing not only the desire, but also the ability, to put a good home-made meal on the table? I know of some who can't thread a needle to sew a button on and would look at you bewildered if asked to darn a sock. As we all know, in the old days the inability to boil or fry an egg caused many men to starve to death. Fast foods have changed all that.

Bacon and egg, by the way, as most English tourists will testify, is now available at many hotels across the Continent and has brought a little more variety into the food displayed on breakfast buffet tables. The bacon is not the real McCoy but it's better than none at all.

***

On the way to the breakfast room we had knocked on John's door in vain. During breakfast he told us that he had risen early for a jog in order to stay in form and to give those in charge a dressing-down for putting him in the room next to the indoor pool. Their excuse had been that it was the only single room overlooking the sea. Nobody had ever complained before. In any case, the ticking-off had worked. They had acquiesced and given him a different room, not below but above road level. We were relieved also to hear that his mother was improving and asked him what his plans were for the day. He, of course, wanted to get behind the wheel again and whisk us off to Palermo. We, on the other hand, after the long drive via Mondello (without seeing the beach), were for a quiet day in a deckchair on the lawn outside our room, relaxing in the warm Sicilian sunshine. It being my birthday, he gave in and, his relocation completed, he went for a swim in the bay.

Alone again, Doris and I decided to take stock of our surroundings. We were in a unique sort of building lying (not us but the building) between the main road and the beach, with two floors above and two below road level. From our room on floor -2 we had direct access to the sea across a strip of lawn some 5 yards wide and beyond that an even narrower pebbly beach. Seen from out at sea, the place must have looked like a Norman fortress. I guess that's how it's meant to look. The first thing we did was to walk around and inspect the building to see where we'd gone wrong the night before. Learning to negotiate the many turnings, we thought, would be good exercise for delaying the onset of Alzheimer's disease and intended to mention it to the lady in black, but we never got round to doing so. Like ours, John's first and third room were on the same level as a very elegant wine-bar and armchair-filled rest room, which opened out onto that already mentioned strip of luxuriant lawn any Englishman would be proud to possess. As you may have guessed, John is hard to please. The second room allotted to him by the management was under the roof. Finding it both hot and noisy, he refused to take it and was finally allowed to occupy a double bedroom on our left at beach level. Having gone to so much trouble to get Doris and me to Trabia, he was not receiving fair treatment, we thought, from Lady Luck.

***

Some people, like me, seem to have been born under a lucky star. Others don't fare so well. On the whole John can't complain, though he's got where he is more through hard work and determination than luck. But another friend of mine, also a hard worker, has been dogged for many years by bad luck. I don't know much about his youth, except that he was 'endowed' with poor health, which over time has resulted in 30 or more operations. Quite a record, I would say.
To get away from home, where, I imagine, life wasn't what it could have been (his parents' marriage ended up in the divorce court), he spent much of his time in a nearby café studying medicine. When I got to know him, he was planning, then already over forty, to open a restaurant in the city, in partnership with a new-found friend, whose aim in life, like his, had always been to one day own a restaurant of his own. Why Steve, a dentist, earning good money, should have wanted to do that is to me obvious. He had spent so much time sitting in other people's restaurants that he had become obsessed by the idea of doing it in his own place. If he and his partner had started off in a small way things might have worked out differently. They didn't!

Expecting a quick return for their money, they invested millions (of Austrian schillings), borrowed from the bank, in renovating the place. Steve asked me to do an English version of the menu. The prices were too high, and I told him so. Untalented cooks and dishonest managers are also often the cause of restaurant failure. In Steve's case all three conditions were fulfilled. Within a year he and his partner were in trouble. They tried to sell the place. Nobody would have it. At the same time the partner, in a business of his own, went bankrupt, leaving him to pay back a massive bank loan. That was bad but only part of the story. Before the restaurant project Steve fell for a Czech woman whose daughter had been to the USA, on a scholarship, and had come back addicted to heroin. He needn't have married the woman but he did. People in love rarely listen to reason and many of us are still not happy with a common-law arrangement. The wedding was in Vienna. Doris and I were invited. It was quite a big affair and everyone was happy, but not for long. Steve and wife moved into a flat near his surgery, leaving the addicted daughter undergoing withdrawal treatment in a Czech clinic. Aware how slim her chances were of beating heroin, he hesitated to have the girl brought to Austria, where treatment would have been much more expensive and, in his opinion, equally ineffective. The result: the girl was discharged from the clinic but didn't remain 'clean' for long. She was found some weeks later in a toilet, dead from an overdose of the drug. The heroin had won! Steve's wife was shattered, blamed him for her daughter's death and took to drink. In Steve's shoes a less well-balanced person might have taken the easy way out. But he stuck it, to be diagnosed a year or so later with Parkinson's disease. Steve is now saddled with a huge bank debt, a sick wife and an illness which for a dentist is more or less the end of the road. Steve is one of millions the gods seem to disfavour.

6. We celebrate my birthday

After ten minutes or so in the water John stretched out on a plastic pallet with a book beside him. We had turned down his offer to take us to Palermo but after an hour or so relaxing in the shade we began to wonder whether we had made the right decision. After all, it was Sunday and perhaps the best day for a trip to the capital. There would be no heavy traffic around, meaning we might even find a parking space. And it was my birthday! Why not spend it in Palermo?

John, naturally, received our change of intent with delight, and one o'clock saw us tearing along the motorway towards the capital. What a difference to the day before! To the right lay the Mediterranean, short glimpses of which we caught, despite the speed, from time to time beyond the trees. (At 140 kph the outside world rushes by too fast for contemplation.) To the left, separating the two carriageways were mile upon mile of oleander bushes. In the North, from where we had come, they were still recovering from a long winter, but here they were already in full bloom. What a wonderful idea, we thought, to brighten up a motorway with flowering shrubs. In Europe's cities many trees, poor things, give in to the stress of traffic, their leaves turning brown when barely open. But these oleander bushes seemed to be thriving on it, or was it the breeze from the sea that kept them free from fumes, if not the noise?

As you approach Palermo from the east the motorway changes to a dual carriageway crossed by numerous roads, all of which, if you turn off to the right, will take you to some part of the city. How we managed, without the map, to choose the right road was in itself a miracle. At the speed we were still travelling a map wouldn't have proved very useful anyway.

"Where do we turn off?"

"No idea," I replied

"You've got the map."

"Correct, but I haven't the eyes of an eagle and my reflexes are not what they used to be."

"You don't need the eyes of an eagle to read a map."

"You do to see the names of the streets, and by the time I've read them it's too late – at the speed we're travelling!"

John didn't slow down until Doris came up with an idea.

"Let's take any one of the streets to the right. Then get out and take our bearings."

As usual, John was less opposed to advice from Doris than from me. At the next crossing the traffic lights were against us. When they came up green again John turned off, and down we went citywards. The gods were on our side: after a few hundred metres we found ourselves in a leafy, park-like area with plenty of space to leave the car.

"This looks a good place to stay," I said. "Lots of trees and no 'Parking prohibited' signs."

"We're no doubt miles from the centre," John replied, but he stopped the car and we climbed out of it. Before we set off on foot I tried hard to memorise our whereabouts, a precaution I have found advisable when parking in strange towns.

***

Until that time when Doris and I sweated blood trying to find our car, parked in a Como/Italy sidestreet, I hadn't attached all that much importance to such a measure. We hadn't left the damned thing for more than an hour! We were on our way from Bergamo to Lago Maggiore and after a snack near the lake spent half an hour or so wandering around. I had been in Como some 40 years before and was amazed at the way the place had changed. Where I had sat, for instance, every day in a restaurant garden near the lake, reading and enjoying the morning air now stood a super-modern hotel, stiffly fenced off from the shore. I must have been so befuddled by the transformation that I completely lost my bearings. Since then, having revisited other, once peaceful, holiday resorts in Europe, I have begun to realise just how alarmingly 'progress' is changing the world for ever. For those of us who know what things were like in the old days it is rather saddening, but come another twenty years and there'll be no one around to regret their passing. So why worry?

We finally found the car in Como, but not until I had raced up and down the promenade several times, like a madman, urged on by

Doris (who also seemed to have lost all sense of direction), and had appealed to a number of locals in excited and therefore very broken Italian for help in locating the small petrol filling station near which we had parked. We didn't make it to Lago Maggiore, not because we were still in shock or anything of the kind, but because the mist that lay over the mountains, shrouding them and the lake and hiding one of the few unspoilt beauty spots still around in Europe, looked like staying put for days to come.

***

We couldn't have chosen a better place to park the car in Palermo. As I have said, the gods had favoured us: through the trees we could see what looked like the wall of a castle. We had chosen to turn into the Via Vittorio Emmanuele, and the structure before us – the Porta Nuova – was one of the more important sights of the city. I would have preferred to give it a quick once-over, but not so my two companions. After our frugal breakfast all they could think about was putting an end to that gnawing feeling inside them. Thinking about it now reminds me of a former friend of mine with whom I spent a month in Paris in 1950. He was a sturdy chap, not what you'd call overweight, but with a bottomless hole where his stomach should have been, and when midday approached his only thoughts were centred on food. If you're well-heeled all you need do nowadays, in Paris, to be sure of a good meal is go into the nearest restaurant. But this was fifty or more years ago, and we were summer students at the Sorbonne, trying to get by on a few shillings a day. Finding an eating place to match our resources was far from easy. Needless to say, most of our time there, when not learning French, was spent locating good but cheap food. Happy memories!

In connection with hunger I have another tale worth telling. In 1970 Doris was found to be suffering from TB and had to spend the first three months of that year in hospital. While she was there I booked a fortnight's holiday for the summer at a well-known Austrian spa. The boarding-house I had chosen was also well-known, though in a different sense, namely for the thrift with which it was being run, but I couldn't know that at the time; from brochures one doesn't learn that sort of thing. I had seen the advert in the travel agency window on the way to my evening school and thought a stay at a spa would be just what the doctor ordered. Strange to say, the specialist who treated Doris after her discharge from hospital recommended the very place (Bad Gleichenberg) I had unwittingly chosen, praising it for its beneficial effect on both lungs and appetite. In hospital, the efficacy of the medication administered and the efforts of the nursing staff had greatly improved Doris's appetite. I was able to cope with her craving for food, from April to June, but the boarding-house, in July, wasn't. Nowadays, wherever you choose to stay in Bad Gleichenberg or anywhere else in Austria you can pile your plate high with whatever you fancy from a rich assortment of ham, salami, cheese and other delicacies spread out on the buffet table in the breakfast room. Not so in the 1970's. In those days you ate what was put before you, and at the boarding-house we found ourselves in it was very modest, by no means enough to satisfy an appetite steadfastly stimulated for 6 months by good solid food. I had chosen a fortnight's stay with full board. After our first meagre breakfast we reminded each other that Continentals tend to start the day with a smallish breakfast, meant rather to whet the appetite for a large repast at midday. We were wrong about that, as also about the evening meal, both of which would have looked less out of place at a beauty farm, where, as we know, the rich obese of both sexes go to shed weight. To cut a long story short, apart from an occasional stroll in the park and surroundings – we had no car in those days – both Doris and I spent the time in between meals staving off our hunger with food from the town's shops – mostly bread rolls halved and eaten sandwich-like with middle layers of salami and cheese. To make matters worse, while sitting on benches in the park we more often than not had to listen to our fellow-spa guests describing to each other the masses of delicious food they were being spoilt with at the many other hotels and boarding-houses in Bad Gleichenberg!

7. Our short stay in Palermo

The trattoria, which I found, by chance, a stone's throw from the Porta Nuova, was one of the highlights of our visit to Sicily. It was a restaurant patronised by locals and the odd tourist fortunate enough to come across it. From the smile on the landlord's face it was obvious that, despite our shorts, in Italy the hallmark of foreigners from northern Europe, he was delighted to be our host. Within seconds he had a table laid for us in a corner near the entrance and was soon regaling us with drinks – mineral water and a local brand of beer, which after lengthy debate, we had condescended to order, not, I may add, with regret.

Doris and I are passionately fond of fish. We had come to the right place for that. John looked on somewhat disapprovingly as we tucked into scampies, fried prawns, octopus, sardines, mussels and the various other kinds of shell fish the Mediterranean still has to offer (hopefully for a few more years to come). John opted for spaghetti or something similar. He used to be a staunch vegetarian and cooking a meal for him still requires considerable forethought. As a youth, like many another misled person, he had got himself hooked on some guru-led sect or other and, for a long time, had been convinced that renouncing meat would promote his spirituality. Then the inevitable happened: he fell out with the boss or the secretary or whoever and was thrown out on his ear. Since returning to relative normalcy he has begun to eat lamb, but fish for him is still a dish seldom savoured.

Doris and I ate our heads off that Sunday in Palermo. After all, it was my birthday and John had proclaimed, in advance, that all expenses would that day be on him. Even as we ate I was, therefore, I suppose, contemplating a similar banquet in the evening. At the other end of the room a birthday was in boisterous progress. If the partymakers had known that I was also celebrating my birthday they would surely have invited us to a piece of the cake they were digging into. Such is the hospitality of the Italians in general and the Sicilians in particular. We finished with red wine, all three of us, and, having taken photos of the interior, sauntered out into the afternoon sunshine, destination city centre.

From somewhere or other John had procured a guide-book to Palermo. We were approaching the fortified wall and archway sighted as we parked the car. We were walking too slowly for our guide.

"Do you want to know about the building ahead of us or don't you?"

During the meal John had controlled his appetite, but Doris and I hadn't and, surfeited, were now no longer so keen on seeing the sights. I couldn't let on how full I felt.

"Of course," I said, "but not here, standing in the sun."

That was as good an excuse as any. Still in the south, the sun was shining straight down the street and there was no shade worth mentioning.

"A little sun won't hurt you."

"All right," I said, "but keep it short."

"I'll read what it says here."

And he proceeded to tell us all about it.

***

We sauntered northwards down the Via Vittorio Emmanuele till, on the left, we came upon what looked like some huge funnel-less liner waiting to sail. A quick look at our guide-book put us right. It was the cathedral. But what were all those people standing in the shadow of the side porch waiting for? Was it a wedding? Or were they planning to attend a church service? We had queued in the old days for food (during the war) or for the cinema but never to get into church. As a boy, I'd queued after the service often enough, impatient to get out, but I'd never queued to get in. Then slowly we realised what the fuss was all about. The people were tourists (like us) intent on 'visiting' the place. They had no doubt been persuaded (not like us) by their local travel agencies that seeing the inside of Palermo cathedral would complete their education and were waiting in the shade for the doors to open. That, we learned, would not be before 4 o'clock, and there were still a few minutes to go. As we stood there, wondering whether to endure the scorching sunshine – there was no room in the shade – I thought of the city I chose to live in 50 or more years ago. Vienna used to be a wonderfully relaxing place to stroll through – few cars, no pedestrian precincts, no tourists, no noise, in short a charming old-world city. All that has changed. Now, more like an outdoor museum, it's a-buzz with holidaymakers from all over the world, brainwashed (by their money-mad local travel agencies) into believing that the buildings erected there in centuries past (by ill-paid labourers) must be seen at all costs, even if it involves flying thousands of miles and thereby producing millions of tons of carbon dioxide. And they come, the holidaymakers, summer and winter, in such numbers as to destroy the very character (and atmosphere) of the place they have been persuaded to visit, filling the city's restaurants and churches and crowding the streets to watch outdoor acrobats and other mediocre entertainers go through their boring paces. Something has gone wrong somewhere. There are others as troubled as I am.

A number of Italian cities, I hear, are considering charging a tourist fee, or are already doing so. "And why not?" You may say. "We pay for everything these days. So why not for the pleasure of strolling past buildings that were put up, a long time ago, not only to live in, but also to please the eye, there being few erected nowadays at home worth looking at."

***

John didn't intend to wait around either. I turned to see him some 50 yards away near the gates, camera in hand, busy recording the scene before us. 4 o'clock came and went, but the doors remained firmly shut, so to while away the time Doris and I strolled round the building – despite the heat. Back at the porch some ten minutes later we found even more people waiting, impatient to get in. For once, John and I agreed: we could 'visit' the cathedral on our way back. So, off we went down the Via, but not far. Doris was thirsty. She would have liked tea, a beverage that quenches the thirst better than any other, but tea with milk being one the Italians, like most Continentals, haven't a clue how to make, we knew it would have to be coffee, at the making of which the Italians excel. In a side street to the right we found a bar with a table or two outside in the shade. Doris and I sat down at one of them and drew up a chair for John, but instead of joining us he chose to sit alone. When we go out together in Vienna he more often than not insists on sitting with his back to a wall and preferably in a corner, so as to face Doris and me and survey the interior and the guests – the girls? – who people it. But he had never before chosen to sit at a separate table. The explanation was not long in coming. From the bag he had carried slung over his shoulder he took out a book, and began to read. Then, noticing our consternation, he explained that he had set himself the task of finishing the book – an amusing story by an English philosopher turned novelist – during the holiday, if not that same afternoon in Palermo.

The coffee drunk and paid for, Doris and I were ready to move on – with or without John. After all, we had come to the capital of Sicily not only to eat and drink, but to see the place, or at least part of it. With a wave of the hand John, engrossed in his novel, told us to go ahead. He would join us, he said, farther down the street. Not wanting to anger him unduly (on my birthday!) we swallowed our disapproval and set off without him. If we kept to the Via Vittorio Emmanuele and didn't go too far there wasn't much chance of our missing him or vice versa. And we hadn't a plane to catch or a hotel to find! Also, I had taken my bearings on leaving the car and knew that if the worst came to the worst I could find it again without much trouble and could rely on his being able to do the same. After half an hour or so we were beginning to think that our visit to Palermo would end that way. How could we have missed him? The Via was a straight street and there was hardly anyone to be seen in it. Everyone was obviously in the city's cathedral or its many other places of worship – keeping cool? After another ten minutes or more spent not knowing whether to be angry or anxious we saw him strolling our way. He had been so fascinated, he said, by the contents of the book that he had lost all feeling for the passage of time. I refrained from telling him that, in my opinion, he had never had any feeling for the passage of time and swallowed my anger. From where we had been waiting at the Quattro Cantoni we continued northwards to the Via Roma and then turned left.

I must admit, the older I get the less interested I become in sightseeing, but how anyone can walk through a strange city without taking the least interest in the buildings around them is beyond me. And when John criticised me for consulting the guide-book more than twice I blew my top for the first, but not the last, time that day. We had come to Palermo to see at least a part of it, I said, and not to read books by English philosophers turned novelists! That took the wind out of his sails, but it also dampened my enthusiasm for Palermo's sights. At the next crossroads we turned left again and walked in silence, me leading the way past the Teatro Massimo then through a labyrinth of narrow back streets and alleys, where cats roamed, women sat, forlorn, in doorways, and children played football, bare-footed, in dusty cobbled courtyards.

Eventually the cathedral came into sight, approached from the opposite direction, and Doris, who had become somewhat discontented, assuming I had lost my bearings, sighed with relief. Two hours or more had passed, and the queue outside the doors had by then long since dispersed. Out of the six o'clock sunshine we strode, unobstructed, into the gloom. I was impressed but not carried away. I had been into too many such places, including, of course, Vienna's equally dismal Gothic cathedral and her countless, sumptuously decorated churches of later date and lesser fame, built, like its palaces, by men who toiled for low reward. Judging by the frequent flashing of cameras all around us many tourists, John included, seemed to find the interior more worthy of recording than I did. I remember thinking of the friends and relatives of all those busy taking photos and the boring time they (the friends and relatives) might well have to spend viewing the results.

***

John's a bit like that: he has a digital camera – one of the latest that he can connect to his computer – and delights in using it. On his many travels around the globe he has taken hundreds of snapshots and videos and, back in Vienna, treats friends and relatives to long showings. I must admit, for a week or two after a holiday it helps pass the time pleasantly to revive one's own memories of happy hours spent away from work and worry, but if you've never been to Bali, say, or Madagascar, or wherever it is you're supposed to go, there are no such memories to revive.

Not long ago I committed the error of wanting to entertain relatives with scenes I had shot while on holiday. Since our time together in Sicily John has bought himself a new digital camera, state-of-the-art with all the latest refinements, and has sold me his 'old' one, the one he took so many shots with in Sicily, on approval, meaning that I can have it cheap if I like the way it handles. People of my age are mostly loath to bother with such new-fangled gadgets. I have, in fact, several friends of my age and younger who refuse even to use a mobile phone let alone a digital camera, or if they possess one, given as a present, haven't the faintest idea how to text you. Or they have mobiles and leave them switched off all the time, which is, I think, very unsociable.

In Istria some time ago I put this new camera to frequent use. Soldiering 60 years ago in West Africa (against my will, of course) I bought a Kodak box camera and took some very good shots with it, photos of a clarity on a par with those produced by many of today's super-efficient gadgets. On my return to England and demobbed, I lost all interest in photography. My lack of interest later became an aversion, due in no small measure to the possession of a camera that played me up by refusing to flash at crucial moments or by turning out blank shots of scenes Doris and I had considered worthy of conservation. John's camera – the one I still have to approve of – is, of course, not a bit like that. It is fool-proof. After shooting a scene you can check whether it's really there and acceptable, which is, I must admit, a big improvement.

I am reminded of the time an old friend of mine – one I used to play cowboys and Indians with 70 years ago – came to Vienna with his wife and a snappy new camera, which he made frequent use of, capturing, under my guidance, some very impressive scenes of Vienna and its surroundings. The couple returned to England, and Doris and I waited in suspense for the postman to bring us the fruits of his and my labour. After a month or so we received the tragic news: we had taken all 32 shots (or was it 36?) with an empty camera! Such things don't happen nowadays, provided you have gone digital.

And that brings me back to the holiday in Istria. Five days after our return Doris and I were invited to a birthday party at a Vienna restaurant run by a Turkish friend of mine. More about him later. 'Invited' is not quite the mot juste because when you are invited someone else foots the bill and in this case we, over-generous as we are, were the ones who did the footing! But that is by the way. In Istria I had tried out John's camera and, carried away by its ease of use and reliability, had taken 50 photos or more, all of them nicely stored and waiting for reproduction. There were 12 people at the long table, six on each side. After a beer I tend to become more talkative. Egged on by Doris, I had taken the camera with me, to use as I thought fit, and handed it round to hear them praise my proficiency, newly gained in Istria. The camera passed quickly from hand to hand, some of the guests not even deigning to look at the photos it contained. No one was really interested in the wonderful pictures I had taken! I put it down, at first, to drink – we had arrived late to a party in full swing – but then I realised I was making the same mistake as John. When it comes to holiday photos most of us are interested, understandably, in reviewing only scenes we have ourselves experienced, with or without ourselves in them, depending on photogenecity, age and current body size, in that order, some degree of obesity now being universally tolerated.

***

From the cathedral we made our way back up the Via Vittorio Emmanuele. The evening before, I had wondered at the number of cars in the streets of Palermo. Compared with what was now happening that had been a mere exercise. On the Saturday the traffic had been moving slowly. Now, as we approached the spot where our car was parked we found ourselves surveying a sea of cars of every shape and size, motionless as far as the eye could see. They were standing bumper to bumper, and we had to cross the road. Were they all off to another football match? On a Sunday? I turned to the right to comment on the situation to John, but he had disappeared. How long had we been walking without him? Had he forgotten where we had parked? Then I spotted him. He was already waist deep, wading through the cars in the wrong direction. As I looked he turned and waved, signalling us to cross. Risking death, Doris and I followed his advice, threading our way carefully to the other side. But where was John going? We didn't have to wait long for an answer. Within minutes of our crossing he had joined us, holding out a bunch of flowers.

"For me?" I asked, it being, as you remember, my birthday.

"Don't be silly!" he replied. "They're for Doris."

Doris's birthday was on the 18th, four days after mine. She was overwhelmed and didn't hide the fact. She kissed him on both cheeks, harder than usual, remonstrating with him for spending his money but loving him for having done so.

"There's more to come," John said, "on the day itself."

"With that he turned and led us to the car."

"You're going to have all your work cut out getting through this lot."

"Don't worry, I've been in worse jams than this. We'll be out of it in no time."

He was right, thanks to the fact that the river of cars had begun to flow again, albeit sluggishly, and to a chivalrous lady motorist. In Italy, as in most countries, there are still a few people around, of both sexes, who, if they have any, retain their good manners when driving. Slowly but surely we progressed towards the motorway. The walk had put my two companions in need again of sustenance, and before long they were discussing the next meal and where it was to be indulged in,

"If you are so hungry, the two of you," I suggested "let's leave at the next slipway, which is Bagheria, and look for a restaurant there."

8. An evening meal in Bagheria

Within minutes we were at our destination with John performing driving feats that had me worried again. When in a strange town in a car looking for a restaurant it's best to drive slowly, and I told him so. In fact, I recommended parking the car and walking. However, hunger seemed to have him in its grip, and he was bent on getting wherever he expected to be fast. The quarrel started when we charged hell for leather down a narrow street (with cars parked on both sides), stopping just in time to avoid entering a   pedestrian precinct. Another yard or two and we'd have ploughed our way through a stream of people enjoying their evening stroll.

"That's what comes of driving too fast!"

"There was no sign to say this was a dead-end."

"There probably is, but we didn't see it because we were – "

"What's wrong now?" Doris chimed in.

"John's bent on killing us all."

"Don't be funny!"

"Other people then."

There was no retort to that. John was already reversing faster, it seemed to me, than we had entered the cul-de-sac. I exploded again.

"For Christ's sake be careful!"

My warning was reinforced by a car hooting some way behind us. John ignored it, backed the car another ten yards and then swung it to the right.

"Didn't you see the chap behind you?"

"Of course, but he's got brakes and saw me reversing."

"Alright, but think of your passengers. You've got Doris and me worried to death."

"Why on earth?" He said. "I know the width of the car and what it can or can't do. You haven't the slightest reason to worry."

I thought of the time he had hit a bus with Doris beside him but refrained from reminding him.

"Alright," I said, "but the sooner we park the car the better."

Fifty yards or more down the street we turned left into an avenue of sorts, also a dead-end, parked the car and joined the people strolling leisurely seawards down the quiet car-free boulevard, happy, I imagined, to be using their legs for walking and not operating pedals or, like me, sweating blood.

Having sat in the back of the car, Doris had missed a lot of the excitement and, once out of the car, raced on ahead with John in search of somewhere to eat, leaving me struggling to calm my nerves. I caught up with them eventually and traipsed around with them for a time before pointing out that it was Sunday and many places would be closed. I was right, of course, as I usually am. We did find one or two trattorias with their shutters down but from outside they looked so sleazy that we wouldn't have wanted to eat there anyway. In the end John suggested we return to the car and try the harbour area. Now and then during our six full days in Sicily John also had a good idea. This was one of them. Long before we reached the harbour, down a still sunny, tree-lined avenue, we were met by the wonderful odour of frying fish.

"This smells more like it," I said, now fully in control and, after so much walking, like Doris and John, also feeling peckish. It turned out to be our lucky day. As we entered the makeshift carpark alongside the quai a car began to leave. In less time than it takes to tell, John had taken possession of the empty space – much to the chagrin of other contenders – and within seconds we were walking towards a larger square, where the restaurants stood side by side vying for guests. We chose one on higher ground in a corner and, while Doris and I studied the large seductive menu, from his usual vantage point in a corner seat John surveyed the scene before us: the boats bobbing in the harbour and the sea still ashimmer in the setting sun. He then reminded me again that it was my birthday and that he was paying for everything, as he would again on the 18th. The thought of fried fish – preferably mackerel or herrings – has always made my mouth water. As we waited to be served, my thoughts went back to the time spent at the army camp of Catterick during the cold winter of 1946. Having completed basic training, we were allowed to go home most weekends. I used to hitch-hike it down the Great North Road (there were no motorways in those days) and on the way stop in Leeds to buy myself a herring or two at Lewis's fish counter.

I also remembered the week spent in Torquay, invited there by a fellow-conscript from my army days in Lagos. Out in Torbay in an outboard motor-powered rowing boat we fished for mackerel, which his mother fried for us. Eat a mackerel within an hour of catching it and you'll never want any other kind of fish!

***

They say the seas will soon be void of fish. There were no signs of that scary prospect in Bagheria. There was fish galore, though expensive. But I wasn't paying for it! So, for the second time that day, Doris and I went to town – at John's expense. I can't remember now exactly what we ate – a mixed dish of every fish, it was, or so it seemed, that the Mediterranean had to offer, helped down with a fruity locally grown wine. It was a memorable meal, a birthday meal (the second that day) I'll never forget. I was quite prepared to forgive John for all the worry and excitement he had put us through during the last two days. I even began to feel sorry for him. After years off meat and fish his taste buds were sadly underdeveloped. Unable to appreciate such delicacies, he again ordered spaghetti and could only watch and wonder as Doris and I tucked in as if we'd had nothing to eat all week. We returned to the hotel about ten and were soon stretched out on the bed, bloated again, reviewing the day's events. We now knew: not for worlds would we have renounced our six-day holiday in Sicily.

9. Off to Cefalu

Locating the breakfast room the next morning proved less difficult for me. Doris, some way behind me, took a wrong turning but soon found her bearings and was beside me before the lift arrived. John joined us later. He had been jogging again – God knows where – and was still in his track suit. Slowly I began to realise why his suitcase was so big: he had the proper gear, it seemed, for every occasion. Thank goodness there was no chance of snow in Sicily or he'd have brought his skis with him and that would have been a nuisance. As we ate, now finally resigned to the frugal breakfast fare, we inquired about his mother and learned, to our relief, that she was still stable, if not slightly improved. That augured well for our week in Sicily. In all probability John would not be called back to Vienna, to leave us stranded in Trabia and faced with the prospect of organizing transport back to the airport when the time came. We also learned that a friend of his, and ours, had already begun the conversion of his mother's bathroom. The bath was to be replaced by a shower and the floor made slip-proof.

**

As I write this I must think of my own present predicament. A fortnight ago, after being shown round a friend's new flat and finally, as the culminating act, led into the bathroom, Doris became obsessed with the idea of re-doing ours. I suppose she's right in wanting a change. All around us people are splurging money on flashy bathroom interiors, with the result that ours, created some 40 years ago is, even for me, beginning to look old-fashioned, if not dowdy. It's not the cost that's got me worried, although that must be kept within limits, but the inconvenience of it all. I had banked on the project being carried out during the summer months, when we could live far away from the noise and dirt in our small summer residence. But unfortunately this nephew of ours, a tile-layer by profession and ready to do the work for nothing (I'm not the only dumb-cluck around) has since informed us that he can't fit our job in until the autumn. This summer residence of ours – my brother used to call it 'The Ranch' – is a wooden structure and poorly insulated. So we'll have the choice of either freezing to death in The Ranch or choking to death in the flat. I think we'll have to go for the former. Some years ago, in the cold season, we had the whole flat redecorated in one go. On such occasions some people choose to stay at a hotel. We didn't! We stayed put during the five-day operation. From the dust and dirt I developed a sore left eye, diagnosed as conjunctivitis by the ophthalmologist, a friend of mine I may later have time to tell you about. He predicted that my right eye would become infected too and that a similar fate was in store for Doris. I laughed. How could he be so sure of that? His prediction was right! Before the decorators had finished Doris had started waking up, like me, with her eyes caked with pus. We both had to resort to eye drops, administered every two hours for over a week! I didn't want that to happen again. Being in hospital, John's mother didn't have much choice as to where to spend the time. She was, in fact, lucky to have a warm and sterile abode while the work was in progress.

***

This was now Day Three of our holiday and, having rested during half of Day Two, John was raring to get behind the wheel of the Fiat again. He had it all planned. We could either go eastwards for the day to Messina, south-eastwards to Catania and Syracuse, or merely southwards to Agrigento. Westwards would only have taken us a mere 30 kilometres to Trapani, a name still fresh in memory, the wrong turn on leaving the airport having taken us half-way there on our first day. Before consenting to any of these day trips we took out a map and considered the distances involved. Messina was 100 kilometres away, Catania 150 and Argentino only 60. We pointed out that we had come to Sicily not only for a change of scenery, but also for a rest, and didn't want to spend the holiday racing around the island in a car. At an acceptable speed Messina and back would mean three hours of the day solid driving and Catania and Syracuse four or five. Agrigento was a stone's throw away and would only take an hour there and the same back, but what was there to see in Agrigento. As in Trabia, we argued, the sea would be blue, the sand brown and the trees, if any, green. Slowly we talked John out of a long car ride and opted for a route that would take us through the National Park via Polizzi, Petralia and Castelbuono to Cefalu, a total distance of some 80 kilometres but, judging from the map, somewhat mountainous. John could show us part of the island and get us back to the hotel before dark. It would also give him an opportunity to test, if not tax, his driving ability. Any fool can cruise along a motorway in top gear. Mountain roads with their hairpin bends and steep inclines are a different proposition, calling for a wheel control and gear-changing skill not everyone possesses. John took the bait hook, line and sinker, with the result that at around eleven o'clock we set off eastwards in the direction of Messina, then south, still on the motorway but with Catania on the signposts.

"We can still go to Catania," John said. "At this speed we'd be there in an hour."

No reply.

"We could also visit Etna."

"Who's Edna?" Doris asked. My wife is hard of hearing.

"We've discussed all this before," I said. "We could go there tomorrow, weather permitting."

"Okay. Where do we leave the motorway?"

"I would suggest at Polizzi. From there to Petralia."

***

The weather was perfect with hardly a cloud in the sky and within minutes – we were travelling fast as usual – we had reached the sliproad. I sighed with relief and settled back to enjoy the scenery, so different from what we were used to in Austria with its verdant valleys and fir tree-covered slopes. What struck me most on that first leg of our trip was the absence of trees and the way the mountains rose cliff-like from parched fields void of cattle or sheep. I hadn't much time, however, to consider the landscape, for the road was beginning to wind and John was enjoying the bends. One remark of his still puzzles me and causes laughter whenever I repeat it to others. We had been chasing another car round the curves for some time when he came out with the phrase: "You can tell a good driver by the way he uses his brakes. The less often, the better the driver." I didn't reply. I simply sat tight and tried to figure out what he meant. Some drivers can't stand having anyone in front of them. John is a bit like that. On a straight stretch of the road we finally overtook the car ahead and settled down to a steady 100 kph, slowing down slightly on the bends. For a while we travelled in silence, until Doris broke it.

"Where do you think we should eat?"

"We're not eating yet for a while. We've only just had breakfast," I replied.

"I didn't have a lot."

"Neither did I" said John.

"Well, I did! What they gave us wasn't very exciting, I'll admit, but there was plenty of it, and we had enough Sunday night to last us a week."

"You did," John said. "You two ate your heads off. I only had spaghetti."

"That was your fault. I keep telling you. Forget your youth and get back to normal food."

That was a reference to his guru-dominated past.

"But if we have a little something soon somewhere, it won't spoil our appetites for this evening."

That was Doris, and what she said was sound reasoning. What could I do? It was two to one. We resolved to find a trattoria or bar or whatever in the next village. The inhabitants of Polizzi, where we searched in vain, apparently never went out for meals. A passer-by told us, in broken English, of a restaurant farther down the road, but it was Monday, he said, and on that day of the week it could be that the place was closed. He was right. I have never seen an emptier carpark. Not that I was worried. In fact I was rather enjoying my companions' frantic and so far futile search for food.

***

Why people can't live happily for more than a few hours with an empty stomach is beyond me. For some reason or other the three-meals-a-day routine has for many become sacrosanct, like some law that cannot be broken. John and Doris are among that majority. I admire all those Muslims who, celebrating Ramadan, can abstain from food from sunrise to sunset, thought I don't quite see how they expect to benefit from practising such self-denial. A friend of mine, a committed Muslim, once said it's so that one can experience what it's like to be poor and hungry. But, from what I have seen, when the sun goes down those same people can't wait to make up for what they've been missing during the hours of daylight. The really poor stay hungry day and night. Incidentally, we Christians used to eat only fish on Friday, no doubt with the aim of pleasing God and being thereby guaranteed unquestioned entry into Heaven or Paradise, or wherever it is people thought they were going and still do.

Talking of Ramadan has reminded me of a Turkish friend I once had, a Muslim, who, like me, despised the mumbo jumbo of the religion he had been born into. The world needs more people like him in every culture. He went with us once to a tavern on the outskirts of Vienna, to Grinzing, where tourists are taken in busloads to sample the food and the wine. We ordered pig's knuckle, one of the restaurant's specialities. It turned out to be much bigger than Doris and I could manage. As I have said, our friend was an enlightened Muslim, advanced enough to appreciate not only a good glass of wine but also pork. We asked him if he'd like to help us finish off the knuckle. Although he had professed to be off his food he accepted. We watched him put it away with those white teeth of his that looked strong enough to tackle even the bone. As he pushed his plate away he said with a grin that he hoped Allah had not been watching him and that it was a good thing he hadn't sinned during Ramadan or his misdeed could have got him into real trouble on the other side. Sadly, he died a few years later, aged 32. Had it been cancer of the stomach I might have thought Allah had been watching him, but it was lung cancer – from smoking? He used to get through two or more packets a day. I reckon the angels would also have blacklisted cigarettes– and for women car-driving – if such vices had been around 14 hundred years ago.

10. John gets lost

The only thing to do was look for a place in the next village. I took out the road map again, for the umpteenth time. We could have chosen between Petralia sottana and Petralia soprana, one down in the valley, the other up in the hills. But I was too slow. By the time I had it sorted out we were past the former and could only hope not to miss the latter. As it turned out, we had already sighted Petralia soprana from afar: it was a collection of houses crowded fortress-like on a hill at a breathtaking altitude. Had there been any cumulus around, it would surely have shrouded them. We had banked on the village, or whatever it was we could see so high up in the distance, being well to the right of our route, but we had banked wrongly. We had to pass through it and were already climbing towards it!

I have been in many Italian towns but Petralia soprana, perched as it is on a plateau 1,000 metres or more high, beats them all for the narrowness of its cobbled streets – all one-way – and the magnificent view of the surrounding countryside. We raced through the village at our usual hell-for-leather speed, thanks also to the relative dearth of traffic, and came to rest in a small square outside a butcher's shop. There are still a few smaller towns and villages around throughout Italy where parking has not become a reliable and lucrative source of revenue for the authorities that run them, but this was not one of those. We took a ticket from the dispenser, placed it behind the windscreen and began our search for food. Luckily – for John and Doris now seemed to be on the verge of collapse for want of sustenance – we found a snackbar round the corner from where we had parked and entered. It was a tatty affair with little to choose from in the way of food. We all opted for coffee with our tramezzini (Italian sandwiches) and looked for somewhere to sit. There was one small table in the corner next to the open door with three rickety chairs placed round it. As usual John took possession of the corner seat and, having ensconced himself in it, from his shoulder-bag took out the book by the philosopher turned novelist and began to read. Obviously he hadn't yet finished it. I picked up a newspaper and for a while, with Doris's help, tried to decipher the headlines. It looked like being a repeat of Sunday's performance, so again, as on the previous day, I suggested to Doris that we take a stroll, in order to give John time for a read, the difference being that he would stay in the snackbar until we returned in 15 minutes' time. Engrossed though he was, we got through to him, and he nodded his assent.

Not wanting to get lost in a strange village, we didn't venture far. Doris and I once lost our way in Venice, and this place looked equally dangerous. So we chose a straight sunbaked road, walked slowly along it for seven or eight minutes, then turned back. Twice seven is roughly a quarter of an hour (15 minutes). I an a stickler for punctuality, a trait that 50 years of marriage has failed to change, and if I agree to be somewhere at a certain time I'm prepared to move heaven and earth to do so. On the dot, 15 minutes after leaving it, we were back at the snackbar. John wasn't there! The car was where we'd left it. We'd passed it on the way back from our stroll, but John had vanished into thin air. Where on earth was he? At school the proprietress had, it seemed, not taken much interest in English. Her command of Italian didn't seem very hot either. Or was it ours that was lacking? We didn't waste much time questioning her. In the shade opposite the entrance to the bar there were two chairs of the same vintage as those inside, if not shakier. They had been placed there, we supposed, for such occasions. We sat down and waited, telling each other that this was what we should have expected and that the English philosopher turned novelist hadn't, after all, such an interesting story to tell as we'd been led to believe. Five minutes passed, then ten, but still no John! After another five minutes my mobile rang. Why it was switched on I'll never know. It was our lost friend calling me!

"Where the hell are you?" I asked.

"I've lost my way."

"You said you'd stay in the snackbar!"

"It was too hot in there. Stop talking and tell me where you are."

"I haven't the faintest idea where we are!"

"Give me the name of the street and I'll find you!"

I gave him the name of the street, inwardly fuming and despondent: the streets were baking in the afternoon sunshine with not a soul about who could tell him how to find us. Why on earth had he gone for a walk if he had promised to wait in the snackbar? And the parking time we'd paid for would soon be up. Both Doris and I were angry, but at least we now knew what had happened. Better said, we thought we did. But miracles still occur. Five minutes later John came into view, red in the face from walking fast in the heat. Before

I could launch into the tirade I had in store for him he held out a small parcel.

"What's this?"

"Happy birthday!" he replied. "Yesterday was Sunday. I couldn't buy you anything in Palermo."

That took the wind out of my sails and Doris's

"We were worried to death," she said.

"Yes, how could you go off like that and leave us waiting around?"

"I thought I'd be back before you returned, but I lost my way."

I didn't know whether to contain my anger or give further vent to it.

"Open your present," Doris said, "and see what it is."

I followed her advice. It was a beautiful ball-point pen – a Waterman's. It must have cost a small fortune.

"You're crazy," I said. "You come to the back of beyond to buy a Waterman's?"

"It's as good a place as any. And it'll help you remember our trip to Sicily."

"If we ever get back alive from it! ......Anyway, thank you very much, but the food I consumed yesterday at your expense would have been more than enough."

"Let me decide that."

"We must get back to the car," Doris said.

We returned to the car, wondering if there was anyone about in the heat of the day out to catch parking offenders. There wasn't! Were we relieved!

More by good luck than good management we found our way out of Petralia soprana – not without taking a wrong turning or two – and were soon on our way northwards along a road that wound for miles through woodland. We were in the National Park!

***

While looking for the way out of the town we had passed a greengrocer`s display of fruit and vegetables spread out, as in times gone by in England and Austria, in front of the shop. At our request John had reluctantly stopped the car. Here we imagined we could sample farm produce straight from the fields. We were wrong, of course. Had it been autumn we might have picked up tomatoes not force-grown in greenhouses but out of doors in the open air or apples that tasted as good as they looked. But it was spring and what we bought proved to be as tasteless as the tack found in the racks of supermarkets Europe-wide.

***

I shall never forget the peaches I ate on my first visit to Italy 50 years or more ago; they were bigger than your fist, much bigger in fact, and you had to eat them with care lest the juice dripped down your chin onto your shirt; or the pineapple we bought once at the roadside and ate in the back of an army lorry on our way to a football match in Abeokuta (Nigeria) in 1948; or the deliciously ripe mangoes picked straight from the tree in that same country. Flown thousands of miles to our supermarkets, pineapples, mangoes and all the other exotic fruits now purchasable can't, of course, be allowed to ripen in the sun, but need juicy peaches and plums be a thing of the past? Like every other fruit sold nowadays they are picked while still far from ripe and stored for months in carbon dioxide or some other gas. Craftily displayed and bathed in light, they look so tempting, but their appearance more often than not belies their contents. I often wonder when we`ll wake up and realise the extent to which we`re being conned. Or are there already too few people around who know what fruit and vegetables can really taste like

11. Through the National Park

On that long drive down to Cefalu I fell to thinking about the man beside me. As I have said, we`re very fond of John despite his foibles (and who has none?). We`ve known him for many years now, ever since he first approached me at school with the request for private tuition. He was in his late teens then, desperate to start at medical school but unable to get through in English. Like that of many another his problem was, I reckon, his failure to realise that it`s sometimes necessary to knuckle under to people in higher positions and simulate reverence when not felt or warranted. As a result, despite above-average intelligence he had failed more than one exam in English and other subjects in his attempts to make the grade at evening school, for him the necessary preliminary to a university education, paid for with money he himself had saved. He joined my class towards the end of his time there, and I couldn't really judge whether he'd been in the wrong hands from the outset or, like many others, had found English too 'easy'. It was probably both. Anyway, he was determined to get through in English and with my help he made it. For a long time I had lost touch with him. Like me he was looking for a deeper meaning to it all and had thought he would find it meditating with a world-famous guru-led sect. This took him to many parts of the world in the company of similarly minded men and women but didn't do much to change his character. I guess we bring that with us from wherever we were before making our début on earth, and nothing – least of all nurture – can alter it.

Then, one day, he turned up in a class of mine, half-expecting me to have forgotten him. I hadn't! He was now working as a houseman at an orthopaedic hospital in the city but was about to set up in his own practice. He had come back at, for me, an opportune moment, for I had developed a so-called snappy finger on my right hand and was undecided whom to chose to put it right. If a believer in such things, you might even say he was heaven-sent: his superior at the hospital, an experienced surgeon, performed the operation, successfully, and left the post-operative treatment to John, who came round several times to our place to change the dressing and resplint the finger.

All that had happened ten or more years before. In the meantime John, a bachelor still, had become an independent GP with his own practice and was doing very well, contributing in his spare time to American and English journals, his aim being to attain a university professorship in General Practice. Doris and I had often been with him to concerts and restaurants, and he had once or twice visited us at our favourite spa, but this was the first time we had undertaken such a holiday together. As we sped down that winding road towards Cefalu I was beginning again to wonder whether we would regret having come with him. We didn't! As Doris and I today still admit, without John's incitement we would never have made it to Sicily and, though we would have preferred to see the island at a more leisurely pace (and without the final act) we wouldn't have wanted to miss it for worlds.

***

Castelbuono proved to be less interesting than the name suggested – a collection of nondescript buildings alongside the main road. Or did we miss the village itself, anxious as we were to reach Cefalu? We got John to stop, but not for long, to allow us to stretch our legs and scan the horizon. Then we were off again seawards. It must have been about five o'clock in the afternoon when we saw the toll-gate ahead of us, We had reached the Palermo-Messina motorway.
"Looks like we're going to have to pay," I said
"There's no one about."
John was right. As we got nearer I realised it must be one of those fully automated jobs where you press a button and wait for the ticket, and my thoughts went back to that time not so long before when Doris and I had driven down to Italy. Taking the ticket from the dispenser on entry to the motorway had been the easiest thing imaginable. It was when it came to paying that the trouble arose. The chap in front had gone through 'with the greatest of ease' and I was expecting to receive the same treatment. Approaching the toll-gate, I fished the ticket out of my pocket and slipped it into the slot, waiting to be told what to pay. The ticket was rejected. The bar remained down. I tried again. The same thing happened. So what the dickens was I expected to do? In the meantime a queue had formed behind me, making me nervous. Then I realised there was no slot there to take money. I must have chosen a wrong gate! This must be one where you simply slip in a credit card or something of the kind. A glance at the mirror showed me I couldn't reverse; the chap behind was too near. It was a hot afternoon and I could feel the beads of sweat forming on my brow. Then, all of a sudden, the bar rose, as if by magic, of its own accord, and I drove through without paying! I had used the Italian motorway without paying! I assume some

76

official had been watching my performance and had taken pity on me, raising the bar electronically from where he was sitting.

But the way that bar rose recalled to mind something similar that had happened a short time before in Vienna. The central heating system in our flat is regulated by a thermostat attached to the living-room wall. Every night before retiring to bed I turn it down. I could set it, of course, to automatic, but we don't always call it a day at the same time. On rare occasions there's a TV show worth watching, which keeps us up till past midnight, and to have the thermostat turn off the heat too early would be uncomfortable. It must have been around eleven on that particular night when I thought it time to turn back the thermostat. The light was on in the adjoining room, with the result that the living-room, separated from it by half-open double doors, was in semi-darkness. As I walked towards the thermostat I began to realise that I would need to switch the light on in the living-room in order to regulate it. I put out my hand to turn on the light, but before I could reach the switch the light went on of its own accord. I was mystified to say the least. But perhaps I should add that it happened not long after that Turkish friend of mine had died in a Viennese hospital of lung cancer. Was he still around in spirit and wanting to assure me of the fact? That sort of thing is said to happen. My friend, by the way, had renewed all our light switches only a few months before his death, so quickly did cancer take him. The only other explanation I could think of was that I had activated that light switch merely by wanting to do so, which, for some people, might seem an even more unlikely occurrence than intervention by the dead.

***

To our surprise the bar was up. The toll-gate, it seemed, had only a short time before been completed and was not yet in operation. We sailed through, decelerating slightly, and were soon rapidly approaching Cefalu. Since leaving Palermo we'd had the road to ourselves. I had been reminded of England in the 1940s before the car-craze hit Europe (or was it before hire-purchase came in?). When you eventually got your new car, after months if not years of waiting, you could take your time driving, uncriticised and enjoying the fresh air and the scenery. On the road that sloped down to Cefalu I was shaken back to reality. We were in the 21st century again with a vengeance: as far as the eye could see there were cars parked, bumper to bumper, on both sides. In my mind's eye I could already see us looking, hopefully not in vain, for a space to park ours. But John didn't seem to be overly worried. He never is. With or without his "Doctor on duty" card, which allows him, in Vienna, to park in places off bounds for you and me, he seems to enjoy scouring the streets for somewhere to park the damned vehicle. Merely thinking of the prospects of entering a town cluttered up with cars makes my heart beat faster, but then I'm much older.

Here and there, as we got nearer the town, I spotted a space or two.

"You're going to have a job parking."

"We'll find a space somewhere."

"Why not park here. We can walk down into the town."

"We can always come back again. And what's a car for if not to get you as near to your destination as possible?"

The answer to that would have been that the car nowadays often fails miserably to get you near your destination, but I kept it to myself. You can't argue about such things with car fanatics, and there's no changing John's mind once it's made up. So I sat tight and hoped for the best. We were running parallel with the shore, and the sea, still some way off on our left, came into view in snatches through the spaces between the shops and houses as we sped down what seemed to be the only approach road to Cefalu. We were still going too fast for my liking and straight for a cliff, it seemed, that loomed ahead of us, a dusky red in the late afternoon sun. I heaved a quiet sigh of relief as our driver slowed down and took the last turning on the left. He had seen the cliff ahead after all! From that moment I began to enjoy the outing again, for within seconds we were entering what I must term a picture-book promenade, where people, obviously holidaymakers, were strolling, carefree, in the balmy five o'clock sunshine. We were all taken by surprise, so different was this from what we had been through in the interior of the island. Impressed, John even stopped the car to survey, with Doris and me, the scene before our eyes. You could have thought yourself at one of the more noble English seaside resorts on one of those rare warm summer evenings of yesteryear, that is, free from the noise of traffic! The only cars in sight were standing parked, one behind the other, along the seaward side of the one-way promenade and – wonder of wonders – there was a space a few yards ahead waiting to be occupied. Within seconds we had parked and were ambling leisurely along the prom with all the other people, the long drive forgotten..

Doris broke the silence. "Why didn't we choose to stay in Cefalu in the first place?"

"Ask John."

John thought for as few seconds, then came out with the reply we might have expected.

"With all these tourists around we'd soon have been hankering for a bit of peace and quiet."

He was right, I thought, though many people nowadays wouldn't share that view, seemingly happy only when filling the decks of luxury liners or sitting side by side on crowded beaches, having flown hundreds of miles, thousands sometimes, to get away from it all.

"I think we've chosen an ideal place in Trabia," I said. "It took a hell of a time to find it, but it was worth the trouble."

John acknowledged that remark with a grateful smile. As we walked I looked to the left at the row of restaurants closely arrayed along the landward side of the promenade and at the waiters standing at the ready to receive their first evening guests. John and Doris were obviously desperate for food and I, too, was beginning to feel slightly hungry. Nevertheless, we defied the tantalising smells that were coming our way and walked westwards past the restaurants, discussing which of them to patronize, spoilt for choice. We had almost reached the end of the promenade when, some way ahead, I spotted a bookshop. To prolong the agony for Doris and John I expressed the wish to buy a book. Living so close to Italy, my wife and I have been down to that country many times and, after years of effort, with the help of a dictionary, I can now actually read Italian. Why the Italians, as a whole seemingly devout Christians, have produced so many interesting books on esoteric subjects is somewhat paradoxical. One could also ask the same, of course, as regards their production of the mafia, but that's a different story. Having myself dabbled, with success, in such diabolic practices – meaning, of course, the paranormal – whenever in Italy I look around for serious new relevant publications, thus killing two birds with one stone, improving my knowledge of the language and bolstering, if not confirming, my belief in a life after death.

In contrast, though from the same parents, my brother Alan, you will remember, was a confirmed atheist (when you're dead you're dead) who didn't want to be cremated! He lost his belief in a Creator, I reckon, in France during World War II when made to repair, for further combat, tanks and armoured vehicles sent back from the front, the remains of their former occupants still inside them. He told me once how he had had to shovel the blood and gore out of them before repair work could begin.

But listen to my story. After the death of his wife Alan bore his solitary confinement, as he called it, for ten years or so with the support of a poodle (which outlived him by a month) and a daily visit to the pub. Doris and I spent four weeks or more with him each year in Bognor and brought him back with us for a five or six weeks' stay at The Ranch, our modest summer residence on the outskirts of Vienna. Alan slept on a pull-out couch in the living-room but would often come into our bedroom to change his clothes and comb his hair (what was left of it) with the aid of the mirror that hung over the electric piano. He admired that mirror and, had we offered to give him it, would surely have taken it back to England with him, despite its weight.

Having chosen to accompany John to Sicily, we postponed moving to The Ranch until the end of May. Entering the bedroom on the first morning after our return we opened the windows and pushed back the shutters to let in the light and the mild spring air.

"Where's the mirror?" Doris asked. I looked. The mirror wasn't there!

"Perhaps Alan's taken it with him. He liked it so much."

"Don't be silly!"

We went closer to inspect. The mirror had disappeared and taken the nail with it, but it hadn't gone far. We found it standing upright behind the piano, intact, with not a scratch on it. We knocked in a new nail and re-hung the mirror. Why had that mirror, after hanging there for well nigh 20 years, chosen to fall from the wall around the time of Alan's death? Was it, as some would maintain, a sort of sign from him?

That sort of thing has often been reported, one explanation being that the deceased person feels the need to convince relatives or friends of his or her continued existence after bodily death. I must admit that a mirror or picture could very well fall from a wall 'by chance' due to nail failure coincidental with a person's demise, but what happened at The Ranch in 2003 could hardly be categorized thus. Let me tell you about it. After a month spent in Bognor we returned at the end of July with Alan for his annual stay with us. We spent the first night after the flight at our flat, then moved to our summer residence at about 11 o'clock the next morning. After fastening back the shutters and opening the windows to let in the warm summer air, we decided to sit down to a cup of tea before unpacking Alan's suitcase. Now, on one of the shelves of the wall unit there stands a battery-operated clock under a glass dome. It has stood there for many years, a present from Alan and his wife, bought in Vienna in the early nineties.

Doris had arranged the cups on the tea-trolley and was standing beside it waiting for the tea to brew before pouring it. As she stood there her gaze wandered to the clock on the shelf.

"What's happened to the clock?" she asked. "The minute hand's missing!"

Our eyes followed her pointing finger. She was right. The clock was still going and from the hour hand we could see it was just after midday, but the minute hand had gone. Doris went closer, thinking that the hand had fallen from the clock and was lying inside the glass dome. It wasn't there! We were more than puzzled. The Ranch had been unoccupied for a month. The clock had been intact when we left for England. Where had the minute hand gone? I can't remember which of us first spotted it lying on the tea-trolley, which had stood a yard or so from the clock throughout our absence in England. Doris picked it up.

"How on earth did it get there? Who's been in here?"

"No one," I said. "The place was locked all the time we were away. Let me have it"

Doris gave me the minute hand and I put it back where it belonged on the clock face, removing the glass dome to do so. In some inexplicable way that minute hand had detached itself from the face of the clock, got through the glass dome and laid itself down on the tea-trolley. But how and why?

"It must be a sign."

Doris's words echoed my thoughts. Sinan, our Turkish friend, had died of lung cancer while we were on holiday in England. We had said goodbye to him at the hospital the day before we left for England, not knowing whether he would last till our return. We had grown very fond of him and he of us. Was it his way of showing us that part of him had survived death? Simply to make a mirror fall from a wall might have failed to convince us. He had needed something more spectacular and had found it! It was the only explanation we could think of. It seemed hardly possible that he had done it before death. He was in too much pain to think of removing a minute hand from a clock and laying it on a tea-trolley. But how did he do it when dead? Had he also switched the light on to perform the feat or hadn't he needed light. Had he perhaps been able to dematerialise and re-materialise the hand? How else, alive or already dead, could he have got it through the glass dome?

When I later went to wash up the tea-cups (my chosen job always) no hot water came through. I called our neighbour round to locate the trouble. A plumber by profession, he soon found the reason: a tap in the hot water pipeline under the sink had, for no reason, been turned off tight during our absence. Our friend had often helped us at The Ranch, turning off the water in the autumn and on again in spring, but that tap had never been touched before.

Bear with me and I'll tell you yet another story, one that has puzzled me for more than fifty years now. This would seem to be a good time to get it off my chest, since it could also have to do with people who have left us for another mode of existence.

It was in the summer of 1953. I had come to Vienna to complete my studies at the university here and during the summer vacation decided to visit Italy. After Rome I spent a few days of my holiday in Naples, one of them among the ruins of Pompei. Outside the gates of the compound there were several stalls where visitors could buy souvenirs. As I looked towards them one of the women standing there beckoned me to come and buy something. I declined the invitation with a shake of the head and continued on my way. But she ran after me and pressed a small, round, metal object into my hand. "If you won't buy anything," she said, "take this with you." I looked at it. It was a medallion bearing the head of the Holy Virgin. I accepted it, at first not knowing what to do with it, for I didn't approve of Mariolatry and still don't. Then it occurred to me that I could give it to the lady of the house where I was living in Vienna (in accommodation arranged by the British Council) in appreciation of all she had done for me, a perfect stranger from a country with which Austria had not long before been at war. She was a practising Catholic. She might even like to wear it on a chain.

On my return to Vienna I told her that I had brought her something back from Italy, a sort of present.

"It's from Pompei, isn't it?"

"Yes," I replied. "How did you know?"

She also knew what it was! She then told me a story that made me very thoughtful. Here it is. Many years ago, before World War II, her parents had been involved in a railway accident on the way down to Italy. Her mother escaped unhurt but her father was so badly injured that the doctors at the Catholic hospital in Udine gave up all hope of saving his life. One of the nuns there then suggested she should pray to the Virgin of Pompei, who had often helped on such occasions. The lady's mother prayed all night for her husband's recovery. To the doctors' amazement he survived his injuries, and as soon as he was well enough, they went down to Naples, to the shrine of the Holy Virgin of Pompei to thank her for her intercession. From Naples the lady's parents brought their daughter back a silver medallion like the one I had been given. After that, the Church of the Holy Virgin in Naples became for them a place of pilgrimage: they went down almost every year to give thanks for what they considered had been a miracle, each time bringing back for their daughter such a medallion as I had been forced to accept. The lady herself suggested that I had been singled out (in England perhaps) to prove to her that her parents were still existing somewhere. She may have been right. Anyway, now she will know. She has been at that other place herself for many years now.

***

The bookshop had nothing to offer in the way of esoteric literature and we were soon back in the street, heading for what we considered the most promising of the many promenade restaurants. We weren't the only ones suppressing our appetites; we could see that many of the holidaymakers were already abandoning the prom to indulge in food. We could also see that many of the hungry had their sights set on the restaurant of our choice, which meant that we would have to scramble for a table and perhaps had a longish wait ahead of us, but if the food was good it would be worth the trouble.

As we sat, patient though smug at having taken possession of one of the best-placed tables, secured so nimbly by John, I couldn't help thinking of the invitation Doris and I had accepted, many years before, in Vienna, to dine with our then future son-in-law in a well-known Greek restaurant. The waiter had been quick to bring the drinks, and with the midday rush already over we were convinced that the food wouldn't be long in coming. We placed our order and gazed around at the luxuriously decorated interior, indicative of successful management, which includes quick service, and reckoned with a wait of some 20 minutes, an acceptable time in a restaurant of that calibre. After sitting there, in vain, for half an hour we began to think otherwise. Had something untoward happened to the waiter? Had he collapsed on the way to the kitchen and hadn't been able to deliver our order, or had he (as once happened to Doris and me) simply gone off home without informing the kitchen personnel that we were there. Our host stood up and wandered off to look for him.

He returned to put our minds at rest. The waiter was still around and in good health. The delay had been in the kitchen, where the cook had been having trouble with the new oven. However, everything was now again under control and our order was being attended to. So we called for more wine and waited. What we talked about to while away the time I can no longer remember, but some of the conversation must have centred on the approaching wedding, that important event in many people's lives that so often ends (as also in our daughter's case) disastrously. When the food was eventually served – an hour or more later – we were so hungry that we could each have eaten a horse, and that's exactly what we thought they'd put before us, except that horse meat isn't served at Greek restaurants. Actually, we had ordered roast lamb, for which the restaurant was renowned, but that was before the Turks populated the country, boosting the 'production' of that endearing (and tender) animal. So what they gave us was probably the meat of a sheep past the wool-yielding age. Add to that the new oven`s misbehaviour, which had led to the meat being on the underdone side, and you will understand why we left that Greek restaurant with aching jaws, vowing never to return.

***

In Cefalu the wait was between the soup and the main dish, that is, for Doris and me, John not having ordered any of the former. He was saving his appetite for some sort of pasta again, which, when it eventually came, some ten minutes before our 'Chef's special' (Doris and I had both ordered the same dish), he devoured in the blink of an eye and had to sit for half an hour or more, watching the two of us wade through ours.

Like my wife I was brought up during World War II and cannot get used to throwing food away. Other people, born later, have few qualms about it and think nothing of sending their plates back with half the contents untouched, because they don't like carrots, or peas, or broccoli, or potatoes, or lettuce, or tomatoes, or whatever it was their parents allowed them to turn their noses up at when they were young. An Austrian friend of ours – brought up during the war in

England – was even taught to "leave a little for Mr. Manners", which she still does. The maxim drummed into me was "waste not want not", with the result that I try never to leave a dirty plate, even now in our western world of plenty, such being the tyranny of habit. But that evening the 'Chef's special' had me beaten. I am also a slow eater. I fletcherise my food, that is to say, I try to chew every mouthful at least 50 times to get the last drop of goodness out of it, which can be very tedious for those with me at table who wolf their food, probably without noticing the taste. Doris got through her 'Chef's special' quickly, probably by spiriting (as she sometimes does) some of it onto my plate while I was looking the other way. As a result, I could not for the life of me finish that main dish, and I fell to thinking, as I often do when struggling to get through a meal, what a unique form of torture it must be to force people to eat more than their fill.

When we called the waiter to pay it was already getting dark. So we strolled along the promenade, this time eastwards with the sea on our left, towards the old part of the town. The shops there, on either side of the narrow streets, looked most tempting, but Doris, like me, was feeling tired after the long drive and the 'Chef's special' and asked John to take us back to the hotel for an early night, which he promptly did, hinting that we could come again to Cefalu before we left the island. The third evening of our holiday thus saw us stretched out on the bed, delightfully replete and looking forward to further similar sensual pleasures the next day.

12. Mondello!

Tuesday was soon upon us. After waking Doris in the usual way – with a kiss – and completing my ablutions, also in the usual way, I stepped out onto the strip of grass outside our room to wait. As to be expected in Sicily in spring, the sky was a brilliant blue and held promise of staying that way. Sunshine is what every holidaymaker prays for, but sometimes one can have too much of it, as we may soon begin to realise even in northern climes. Since our visit to Sicily 'climate change' has become a household word, thanks to the fact that those at the top have, at last, begun to understand that they, too, will pay the price. Already 30 years ago it must have been apparent to even the dimmest of us that the proliferation of the motor-car and aeroplane would change the composition of the air we breathe. But there was money to be made from the two inventions, and we took full advantage of the pleasures they offer, regardless of the consequences. I reckoned with a deterioration of the earth's atmosphere and an increase in the incidence of respiratory diseases, but what is actually happening seems to be of a direr nature. In the 1960's, as a teacher of English, I occasionally offered my pupils the composition topic 'The motor-car – The devil's invention'. None of them ever attempted to write on the subject. They simply smiled, puzzled that I should have had such a strange idea. I wonder what those pupils, now grown to manhood, think. Are they still smiling? I doubt it. Some of them may even share my and other fellow-pessimists' opinion, namely that, unless the motor-car, the invention that more than any other has promoted our worldwide economic upswing, is not quickly and appropriately modified, it will soon lead to worldwide disaster.

***

On that third morning in Sicily we could have found the breakfast room with our eyes closed – turn right on leaving the room, then left, then right, then left again and the lift is on your right, enter lift, press button, exit lift, pass reception, enter second lift, exit lift, turn right (or was it left?) and you're there! 9:30 saw us already (or was it finally?) hustling for food. We also knew where everything – salami, cheese, butter, etc. – was and were soon seated, actually enjoying the mediocre 3-star hotel breakfast fare we had before us. Even I was hungry again, despite the previous day's orgy. Doris, however, was again having trouble with the tea. A former coffee fan, under my influence she has become addicted to tea (with milk, not lemon) and prefers it strong. On holiday, knowing how small the chances are of getting a good cup of tea anywhere, I take to drinking coffee. Not so Doris. In fact, she always has her own tea bags (now sent from

England) with her and hopes for boiling water. Difficult to procure at all times, half an hour before breakfast ends at a 3-star Italian hotel boiling water is a commodity surely not to be had for love or money. We were wrong. The water in the urn was less than luke warm, and the two tea bags Doris had dropped into the cup had hardly coloured it. But while we were considering the next move John turned up, in his track-suit again, listened to Doris's lament for a second or two, then went into immediate action. Picking up her cup, he marched off into the kitchen. I looked at Doris and shrugged my shoulders, meaning, "What's the use? He can't speak the language." I had underestimated John's linguistic ability. Two minutes later out he came with the cup in one hand and a shining jug of what proved to be scalding hot water in the other.

"How did you get that?" I asked

"I made love to one of the waitresses."

I knew which one. He'd had his eye on her from the start and had commented on her shapely legs.

***

Incidentally, Doris and John are not the only Austrians I have converted to drinking strong tea with milk. People over a certain age who come to me to learn English are given the choice between coffee and tea. Those who choose the latter soon recognize its superiority as a beverage, a fact also recently confirmed by laboratory tests. And that brings me to an incident worth relating, if only to underscore what tea can mean to the English. A team of workers had come to prune the sycamores in our courtyard. While they were lopping off the lower branches a pupil arrived for an English lesson. He was late and it was long past breakfast time, which, if I remember correctly, had been a makeshift affair that morning. As a result, I was longing for a drink of something again, preferably tea. Now, we live on the ground floor and, it being spring, the door between hallway and courtyard was open wide to let in the warm air. Horst, my pupil, had become a tea enthusiast, so while letting him into our flat I called out to Doris, in the kitchen at the time, to put the kettle on. I had hardly closed the door when a knock came at it. I opened it. Standing outside was one of the tree pruners.

"Did I hear you say *Put the kettle on*?" he asked in English.

"You did," I replied. "You must be an Englishman. Would you like a cup of tea?"

"Can a duck swim?" was his reply. "Two, please. One for me and one for my mate."

We made the tea extra strong that morning, perhaps to impress him. As I handed him two mugs with milk and sugar, on a tray, I told him how long I'd lived in Vienna – more than fifty years. He was dumbfounded.

"How come you speak such good English," he asked, "after 50 years in Austria?"

"I teach it," I said. "We have a garden in the outskirts. Show me how to prune trees and I'll teach you German."

He laughed. I didn't get round to teaching him German. I didn't even ask him his name or which part of England he came from. I had a pupil to teach and he (the pruner) was soon being hoisted up one of the trees, where he was still poised when I went off to my weekly massage. From the empty cups (Had they been licked clean?) we gathered that they had enjoyed the tea, probably the best they'd had in weeks.

***

On Day Four John had been jogging again and, like us, was ready, it seemed, to eat anything, putting away more bread in five minutes than I could eat in a day. He had also been in contact with his family in Vienna: his mother was still improving. That had put him in a good mood, of course, and he was eager to undertake a new trip somewhere, about which we then began to deliberate. We should get away earlier this time, he thought. No messing around in the hotel grounds or going back to bed for a nap, something Doris and I like to do when on holiday alone. After discussing at length the pros and cons, from the medical point of view, of resting after a meal, John condescended to allow us an hour on the bed, during which time he would go for a swim in the bay. We therefore repaired to our respective rooms, agreeing to be ready for take-off in an hour's time. Doris said she was still tired from the previous day's drive, or did she also want to process the impressions of that second full day of the holiday? In any case, whether good for you or not after a meal, sleep had soon enfolded her in its arms. I had taken a number of books with me. I always take books with me on holiday. Too many in fact. Most people take too many clothes with them, half of which they never wear. I take too many books, half of which I don't read.

I probably spent several minutes looking for my reading glasses, for whether at home or on holiday with me they never seem to stay where I put them. It's been like that as long as I can remember. People who don't yet need glasses for reading or who do but keep them on their noses or hanging round their necks all day have no idea how elusive a pair of spectacles can become. The fact of the matter is that we do so many things without thinking, and laying glasses down when not needed is one of the most frequent. All in all, I must have spent many weeks of my life looking for my reading-glasses. And I have found them in the most unexpected places – in cupboards, drawers, bookcases, in arm-chairs, raincoat pockets, in Doris's handbag, under the bed, in the garden even, where they have lain for days on end among the rose bushes, forcing me, more than once, to borrow my wife's. Some time ago, in desperation, I bought myself a second pair, but that, of course, has only made things worse: both pairs now frequently get mislaid. Before Doris became far-sighted and found herself plagued by the same problem she used to tell me, repeating a comment often used by my mother, though in connection not with glasses, but with articles of clothing, mostly socks or shoes, that I would lose my head if it were loose. And John has told me often enough to get myself a pair of bi- or even trifocals and wear them all the time, as he does, but I feel I am not destined to enjoy such high-tech blessings. The pair of bifocals, bought some years ago at considerable expense, slipped out of my shirt pocket as I was climbing over a fence. I jumped onto them, stamping them firmly into the soil. The trifocals, purchased a few years later and even more expensive, served me for a short time only, an eye operation rendering them useless a month after I'd bought them. With cataracts now waiting to be removed from both eyes I am looking forward to a future free from spectacles, but who knows?

***

One of the books I had with me, I remember quite clearly, was 'The Clash of Civilisations', bought at Heathrow Airport in April. It was hard going and depressing and made me think again of the situation back home in Vienna, where, as in other European cities, we are being overrun by people from a very different culture, intent on retaining their identity, and are doing next to nothing about it apart from forcing them to learn the language.

I read for half an hour or so then left Doris sleeping and stepped out into the sunshine. John had also been reading, some way away on one of the many plastic loungers stacked for the use of hotel guests. As I looked towards him he was taking off his shirt, preparing to go for a swim. He saw me and waved. I waved back. He beckoned to me to join him. I thought for a moment, then went back into the room to put my swimming-trunks on. Doris was still asleep. When I returned to the beach he had disappeared! Two or three small fishing boats were bobbing in the bay. For a moment I thought he might be hidden from sight behind one of them and watched, expecting him to come into view. But he didn't. Then I spotted him out beyond the breakwater and waved. From his antics it was obvious he wanted me to join him, but for me the distance was too far. I could have got out there easily enough, but I would have to get back again.

I remembered what had happened to my brother, my age at the time, in Turkey three years before. Our Turkish friend, Sinan, had taken us on a boat trip, complete with a fried-anchovy lunch and an opportunity to swim. With the ship at anchor, the three of us chose to swim to the shore of the island some 200 yards distant. We reached land easily enough, but I could see that getting there had taken it out of Alan and, looking sideways at him from where we sat on the sand, I was beginning to doubt whether he would make it back to the ship. My fears were confirmed. On the way back the strain proved too much for him and he began to gasp for help. Our Turkish host, a powerful swimmer, took him under one arm and virtually carried him back to the boat.

John is also a good swimmer, but could he save my life in that way? I decided not to put him to the test. I ventured into the water, which could have been warmer, considering it was the Mediterranean, but kept within easy distance of the shore, thus reaping John's scorn when we finally met again on dry land.

"I thought you were a good swimmer."

"I was a good swimmer when I was your age. And the water's too cold."

He had no answer to that. He was shivering.

"You went out too far," I said.

"Nonsense. It wasn't more than half a kilometre."

"It was beyond the breakwater."

"So what?"

"So what if a shark gets you?"

"There aren't any sharks in this part of the world."

"I wouldn't be too sure of that. And who's going to get us to the airport next Saturday if you're eaten by sharks?

I had often thought about getting to the airport on our day of departure. If John's mother were to take a turn for the worse or even die would he want to return immediately to Vienna?

"If the sharks get me you can take a taxi from the hotel."

"If we do that, there's one thing we can be certain of."

"And that is?"

"The driver won't go via Mondello."

"Okay. I shall never hear the last of that."

"I'll make a pact with you," I said. "If I die before you, which is most likely, seeing I'm 30 years older – "

"Thirty-five."

"If I die before you and you try to contact me, my identifying word will be Mondello."

He laughed. We had often talked about such things.

"Agreed! Now, have you decided where you want to go?"

At that moment Doris joined us. We all sat down to deliberate. We didn't want to go far and finally opted for Monreale, where, for Doris and me, there were one or two things of interest to visit. We lost no time getting ready and half an hour later were on the motorway travelling rapidly westwards. I had the map of Palermo on my lap and was trying feverishly to work out exactly when to turn left, when John said something that made me smile.

"If the car had a GPS it would make finding places a darned sight easier."

"Provided you know where you want to go."

"You're not referring to Mondello again?"

"No, I'm thinking of Klagenfurt."

***

Klagenfurt is in Carinthia. It had happened the year before. While spending a restful week on one of the many lakes in that province of Austria, John had learned by phone that on our way down to Grado Doris and I were intending to stop over in Pörtschach, a well-known holiday resort on Lake Wörth, the place, incidentally, where Brahms put the finishing touches to his violin concerto. Since the return to Vienna would take John past Pörtschach he had suggested breaking his journey there, in order to spend a few hours with us. We agreed and gave him the address of our hotel, which was situated over a mile from the town on the hillside overlooking the lake. He arrived, as planned, on our first morning there, and the three of us sat for a while on the sunny slope admiring the spectacular scene spread out before us – Maria Wörth on the far side of Lake Wörth, the wooded slopes behind it and the mountains towering in the distance.

It was Friday and John had to be back in Vienna that night. He had agreed to join friends for a sailing holiday on the Aegean the next day. The plane for Thessalonika left at 10 a.m., but as it would only take him four hours or so to get back home and all he had to do was throw a few things in a suitcase, he suggested a stroll along the lake followed by a meal at a lakeside restaurant. We would go in his car and he would then bring us back to the hotel before continuing northwards. We left the car in a restaurant carpark and strolled leisurely for half an hour along the footpath at the side of the lake, returning, equally leisurely, to the restaurant for a meal. It was so pleasant to know that a few days free from worry were ahead of us. John was probably enjoying the same feeling. Little did he know what was immediately ahead of him – and us.

For Doris and me everything was new, but John had been there before and knew the town like the back of his hand. We had a good meal. Then, it being only 2:30, we accepted John's offer to show us round the place before leaving. There was even talk of his coming back to the hotel to drink a cup of coffee with us. As we walked away from the lakeside carpark, intending to return later for the car, I happened to glance to the left.

"There's the post office, Doris," I said. "Now we know where to post the cards when we've written them."

"That's not the post-office," John said. "It's a bank." Then he added, almost shouting, "Good Lord! I've forgotten to draw the money out."

"What do you need money for?"

"For the holiday in Greece."

"Well, draw it out now. You have half an hour before the banks close."

"But my bank's in Klagenfurt."

"Klagenfurt's five miles away. Get the money from a cash dispenser in Vienna."

"No go. I have to transfer some from my savings account."

"We can lend you money. How much do you need?"

"4,000, at least"

"John needs €4,000 for his holiday in Greece."

But, being deaf in one ear and half deaf in the other, Doris didn't hear me. She had separated from us and was admiring the display in a shop window.

"It's now 2:35. We can be in Klagenfurt in less than 10 minutes. You can come with me, and I'll bring you back to the hotel."

"Where's John off to?" Doris had seen him hurrying back the way we had come.

"He's taking us to Klagenfurt with him."

"He's what?"

"You heard. He's taking us to Klagenfurt in the car. He needs money and his bank is there."

"But we don't have to go with him to Klagenfurt?"

"What else can we do? Wait here till he comes back? He'll take us to Klagenfurt and bring us back to the hotel."

"But he has to be in Vienna this evening."

Before I could reply John was beside us with the car. He was in a hurry. We climbed in reluctantly and within minutes were racing along the motorway, destination Klagenfurt.

"What are we looking for?" I asked.

"Bahnstrasse. We'll be there in no time."

At the speed we were going I was prepared to believe him. He was holding the wheel with one hand and keying the name of the street into his GPS with the other. By the time the voice came through, a pleasant female voice full of self-assurance, we were already in the outskirts of the town with the centre not far away.

"Take the next turning right."

John took her advice and within seconds we were racing down what was obviously a main street.

"Take the next turning left," the lady said in perfect English, "and you are at your destination."

John switched her off. What a wonderful invention I thought, but one has to be very attentive and drive more slowly when in a town. The next turning left was immediately after the railway bridge under which we had just come, but we were travelling fast. Our driver was in a hurry to get to the bank. It closed at 3 p.m. and it was now 2:50.

"You've missed it," I said. "That was the street we wanted, straight after the bridge."

"I think it was the street before the bridge," Doris said.

"So do I," John replied.

"Whichever it was, we missed it. Turn the car and let's go back."

Instead of doing a U-turn, which was probably prohibited anyway, he turned left down the next side-street, then left, then left again. He had the right idea except that it was taking longer. We turned right to the railway bridge and went under it, then turned right again. The time was 2:52. But we weren't in Bahnstrasse. We were in a kind of loading yard where several trucks were standing around.

"What do we do now?" John asked.

"Get us out of here. Switch your lady-friend on again," I said. "She got us into this mess. Perhaps she can get us out of it again."

John reversed, switched on his GPS and keyed Bahnstrasse in again. The voice came through loud and clear, as confident as ever.

"Take the next turning right."

She didn't seem in the least perturbed that we hadn't found what we were looking for and continued to hand out instructions.

"Take the second turning left."

"Aha!" I said. "I was right. We're going back to Bahnstrasse, where we've already been."

We turned into Bahnstrasse, but it was not the kind of street you'd expect a bank to be in.

"You have reached your destination," the lady informed us.

"If this is a bank I'm an Irishman."

We had stopped outside a clothes store or something similar.

"Perhaps the bank has moved," Doris suggested.

"It's certainly not here," I added.

The time was 2:55. Pleased with herself that she had brought us again to our destination, John's lady-friend had fallen silent. It was then that John had one of those brilliant ideas of his. He lowered his window and addressed an elderly gentleman who was crossing the street from the other side. Had he been a tourist we'd probably still be looking for John's bank, but he wasn't. He was a native of the place and, luckily, though a little deaf, a man of few words.

"What did you say you were looking for?"

"A bank," John replied. "Bawag. Bahnstrasse – "

"Oh, the Bawag isn't in Bahnstrasse. It's in Bahnhofstrasse."

"Bahnhofstrasse?"

"Yes. You go under that bridge and take the second on the right. That'll bring you straight to the Bawag."

The man was heaven-sent, but John was slow to realise it. Before turning the car he keyed in the new destination, and the voice came through again immediately, as unruffled as ever. We were nearing the railway bridge again.

"I got the street wrong," John said.

"We'd gathered that."

"Take the first turning right," the voice said.

"Switch that damned thing off," I said. "We know how to get there."

John was undecided. I could almost feel him thinking. Whose advice should he take? The man's or his girl-friend's? The time was 2:56. We were under the bridge now for the third time.

"Take the first turning right," the voice said.

"That man said the second turning right."

John wavered, then opted for the man, but he didn't switch his girl-friend off. She, in the meantime, had grasped the new situation.

"Go straight ahead and take the first turning right."

"I can see the bank," Doris said as we turned the corner. She was right. It was just ahead of us on the right-hand side.

"You have reached your – "

John had switched her off. The time was 2:57. Lady Luck was smiling. There was a space waiting for us was next to the steps. All John had to do was scramble out of the car and run up them. The bank employee who greeted him was obviously delighted to see him enter the bank three minutes before it was due to close, for she kept him in there a long time. Or did he keep her? It must have been 3:15 when he finally emerged through the glass doors, obviously in possession of the money he so badly needed for his holiday in Greece. We were somewhat disgruntled, not without reason, we thought, but John soon put us in a better mood by suggesting a stroll through the town centre. A few minutes later we had parked near the square where the famous dragon stands and started taking photos with our camera, the one that had so often played me up in the past. The results were predictable. John took a shot of Doris and me standing next to the dragon and I took one or two more of Klagenfurt but, as usual, they were all blanks. John drove us back to the hotel in Pörtschach, as promised, but he didn't stay for coffee. On Saturday evening he texted me from Greece. We were pleased to hear that he hadn't missed his plane.

***

We were now entering the outskirts of Palermo and would soon have to turn left at one of the major crossroads. Inevitably, at the speed we were travelling we missed the turning.

"That's where we should have turned left!"

"Don't worry there'll be another opportunity."

But there wasn't!

"Mondello's on the signposts. Let's go there."

My guess was that he'd wanted to go there all along and had deliberately missed the road to Monreale.

"All right. We've heard a lot about Mondello and we've been through it – fleetingly. Let's now have a look at the place. What do you say, Doris?"

Doris didn't mind the change of plans, and Mondello being well signposted, probably for drivers like John who like to get places fast, within minutes we were entering the area the name of which I shall, for obvious reasons, never forget. We drove in from the south and turned left onto a hot, sunny promenade similar to the one in Cefalu but much wider and longer. The sea was on the right, houses, in their own shady gardens, on the left.

"Why didn't we come to stay in Mondello?" Doris said.

"Ask John."

"I thought this was the place we were coming to."

We all thought that," I said. "Perhaps next time – if there is a next time."

It was midday already and we had to rid ourselves of the car somewhere.

"Let's park the car and get out."

For a change John did exactly what I suggested. After some 200 yards we turned left from the promenade and found a shady spot down a side-street. As in Cefalu I was impressed by the un-Italian surroundings. I stopped to admire them.

"Wonderful!" I exclaimed. "With all these trees around you could imagine yourself in England on a sunny summer's day."

But John wasn't listening. Neither was Doris. They were already walking towards the promenade. I caught up with them.

"What do we do now?" I asked. "Sit on the beach or walk around a bit?"

"I may go for a swim," John replied.

"You spent the morning swimming."

"Okay, then I'll just lie in the sun."

We had reached a break in the railings, where steps led down to the beach. In contrast to other Italian beaches, where I have seen people, lots of them tourists from other countries, lying side by side like sardines in a tin, this one was only sparsely patronised, but there was nevertheless a good sprinkling of well-endowed girls in scanty swimsuits, a fact that had obviously not gone unnoticed by our friend, a bachelor still and free to strike up a conversation with representatives of the fairer sex when and how he wished, which he sometimes does, with success, in our presence, leaving us to do our own thing. Not that we mind, being much older and thus forbearing. Aware of the hazards of such casual pickups, I have more than once, without success, advised restraint.

***

When John left us, as he did, to our own devices I was reminded of the fortnight I spent in Czechoslovakia many years ago. It was in 1950, when the country, recently a victim of Soviet expansion, had organized a youth rally to convince young people worldwide what a wonderful idea communism was. After my father's untimely death my mother had married and settled down in London with a Czech national who had served in the Free Czech Army. Through his mediation and a visa obtained, more by luck than good management, from the Czech embassy in Paris (while with my hungry friend) I was able to spend two weeks of the summer vacation in Prague with the only one of his four brothers (and family) who had not been exterminated by the Nazis – by being married to a so-called Aryan! I was then 22 years old, he, Leopold, in his mid-fifties. To show me more of the country, then "prospering under communist rule", he suggested a trip to the source of the River Elbe, which begins as a small spring in the Giant Mountains near the Polish border. During the hike we picked up with two girls of about my age. They were not only pretty but, as it turned out, of seemingly easy virtue. My step-uncle enjoyed their company immensely, for they also spoke Czech, which I didn't! For most of that strenuous uphill walk to the source of the Elbe I was left to my own devices, but I took it in good part, realising what a miserable time he must have been having with the woman who had saved his life. She was a confirmed hypochondriac. I wouldn't want to swear to it, but the man I saw disappearing with the two pretty girls into their hotel room on that first night of our tour looked very much like my stepfather's brother. I was tired to death after the climb. How he, over fifty, found the energy for such an escapade is beyond me.

***

When John suggested separating for a while in Mondello he was, of course, looking for young female company and, as we could see, there was plenty of it around on that famous, sunny beach. I had spotted a bookshop and Doris was hankering for a drink of something somewhere, so we let him go willingly, arranging to meet again in an hour's time, long enough, it seemed, for him to strike up an acquaintance.

 For me the bookshop proved sadly lacking, with the result that Doris and I spent most of the hour in the garden of a snackbar over a cup of weak coffee. Instead, we could, of course, have strolled around the town. Why that didn't occur to us I can't think, unless it was that we'd heard the name Mondello too often and wanted, deep down, to forget where we were. It may also have been its similarity to other resorts of its kind. When you've seen one you've seen them all sort of thing. There's the sea, a beach, a promenade, shops, restaurants, a funfair and disco perhaps and that's it.

***

Before leaving the snackbar I paid a visit to the toilets. I often do that in a strange restaurant. Not always to use them, but out of curiosity, to give them the once-over, so to speak. A restaurant's toilets are

100

often a sign of success or failure. And I must say, I have come across some very fanciful toilet interiors in my time – luxuriously tiled and fitted out with all-automatic urinals and washbasins, hand driers or paper towels for those men who bother to wash their hands, automatic doors for those who don't, and so on. Some toilets are so attractively and interestingly designed that, more than once, I have felt reluctant to leave. Money invested in such luxury, of course, puts food prices up but not necessarily the quality, which, theoretically, should have been the reason for the innovation in the first place. There's a lot of money to be made, incidentally, catering for that human need. As we all know only too well, the cost of answering the call of nature when on the road has risen disproportionately, compared, that is, to that of satisfying our other basic needs. On the German motorways it has become, like the teaching of English (which is not taught on the motorways), big business, dwarfing the profit made, I would say, from the sale of food. Woman or man, whatever your need – number one or number two, or both – you join the queue at the slot-machine and pay to get through the turnstyle. Dodgers don't stand a chance.You either pay and get through, or solve the problem elsewhere. But what profession doesn't exploit some human need? Can you blame anybody for wanting to cash in on this one. Dogs are, of course, not allowed through but toddlers are and, if you have decided to have children instead of a dog (or dogs), you can change their nappies free of charge.

***

We reached the break in the railings and saw John on the sands chatting up a young lady in a black swimsuit. He had stripped off to the waist but was still in his shorts, so had not been for a swim after all. He hadn't gone far to find what he was after. John's English is good enough to make anyone interested in the language ready to converse, if only for a bit of practice. The two of them seemed to be hitting it off well enough, or was she only pretending to be interested? As we stood there at the railings he turned, as if sensing our presence, and waved to us to join them on the beach, but we declined. Reluctantly, it seemed, he took leave of the girl and came

101

up to us, shirt in hand, turning as he did to wave goodbye. She reciprocated, then went back to the job of acquiring that attractive though often misleading suntan women (and men) like to sport.

"You could have stayed there," I said.

"Yes, but I'm hungry and she's leaving soon anyway."

We were hungry, too. It was getting on for 2 o'clock. We decided to walk westwards away from the town centre to where we could see restaurants lining the landward side of the promenade.

"She looked very nice," Doris said.

"Yes, she's all right. Lives in Mondello."

"What language did you converse in?" I asked.

"English, of course.... She comes down to the beach every day."

"So we know what's on the cards for tomorrow."

"I said I might come by."

"Where can we eat?"

Doris had prevented me from ragging him further. I would probably have warned him not to forget his condoms. In answer to which, if he weren't a doctor and didn't know me better, would, no doubt, have asked me to lend him one. Actually, John is very broad-minded in that respect and can enjoy a smutty joke. He also likes a good limerick. In fact, he and I once tried translating one into German. It was the one about that naughty lady from Crewe, but limericks are, of course, untranslatable and the result was pathetic to say the least.

"That looks a likely place."

I pointed in the direction we were walking, to the last of the restaurants near the headland that formed the western limit of the bay. All but one of the tables in the garden outside were occupied.

"If we hurry," I said, " we'll get the last free table."

We were lucky. I put on speed and got there first, forcing a less fortunate group of four to look for accommodation inside. It had been a long walk from that break in the railings, and we were glad to be sitting. I had offered John the best seat with a view of the part of the beach from where we had just come. He was very thoughtful. Perhaps he was thinking about the rendezvous next day and how he could best turn on the charm when he met her. Despite the crowded restaurant we didn't have to wait long for the menu, a huge affair with hundreds of dishes to chose from. No wonder the place was so full of holidaymakers busily enjoying their food, some more noisily than is proper for people in a civilised society. But, then, if you eat out a lot, as we do, you tend to realise that not everybody in Europe has learnt good table manners.

It was fish again for Doris and me, but John was still holding back. In Vienna, thanks maybe to our influence, he will, now and again, give fish a try (preferably plaice and well done!), but in Italy he steadfastly refrained. Perhaps he was worried about a recent oil spill and the danger of contamination. On the other hand, it may only have been the hangover from his vegetarian past that made him so wary. That day, he went for a pizza of all things! In the old days, before some bright Italian spark had the idea of decorating it (sparsely) with sundry titbits, the pizza was a 'poor man's dinner', eaten with a thin covering of tomato purée. Now it is the fast food par excellence! With the possibility of such maritime delicacies and the speed at which the people around us were enjoying them Doris and I could only smile about John's choice. One thing's for certain. If the supply of fish gives out – and that's the way things seem to be going, thanks to refrigeration and fast transport – John will not have contributed to mankind's predicament.

While we were waiting to get 'stuck in', a coach pulled up outside in the street. It was loaded with what must have been people from a twilight home or similar institution, for every single one of them needed the assistance of the guide and driver, who, after lifting them out of the coach, helped them to hobble into the restaurant next to ours. They were Germans, women and men, most of them with one foot, if not both, already in the grave, enjoying what was for many, possibly, their last holiday. Could one blame them for wanting to spend it in the Sicilian sunshine? But for the grace of God, who has allowed Doris and me to remain agile into old age, and our friendship with John, who likes us so much, we would have had to travel in a similar way to see this wonderful island. Which of those men and women struggling out of that bus hadn't a moving tale to tell. Which of them hadn't been, like most of us, through the mill? And what, I wondered, was round the corner still for my wife and me?

***

I thought of those who had been close to us and what they had been through. Doris's mother, for instance. She'd had a hard life: married at 15, a son abducted by the Russians, twice a refugee from today's Moldavia with her ten-year-old daughter, a husband declared missing for fifteen years, then proclaimed fallen....... When the time came, we thought she deserved something better than a twilight home. She had lived alone for 30 years or more. Then, at age 75, when too much television and a wrong diet led to hallucinations and a violent quarrel with the lady next door we acted swiftly, taking her (Doris's mother, not the lady) to live with us. Caring for her wasn't always easy, especially towards the end when incontinence set in, but we know we did the right thing. She died, age 85, in the ambulance on the way to the hospital.

My mother fared slightly better. She lived to the ripe old age of 92, in her own house, the last two years alone, and passed away in bed waiting for her nightcap, a cup of tea, to be served by the lady employed to care for her. The ten best years of her youth she spent nursing her first husband, my father, who suffered from multiple sclerosis. Then, happily married again, she developed polyarthritis and needed an electrically operated armchair to sit her down and stand her up. My stepfather waited on her hand and foot as long as he could, until he was called away, two years before her.

Hunted first by the Nazis, then by the Communists, he had been ill-favoured by Fate from an early age. As if not punished enough for being a Jew, he fell into Lady Luck's disfavour again when in his dotage. After retirement he developed a disorder that had the doctors baffled, caused, I firmly believe, by slipping on a banana skin, thoughtlessly thrown down at Victoria station. He had been wearing a thick overcoat at the time but he fell on his back and probably damaged his spine. He was over seventy when this trouble of his began. If he started to sway when you were with him you could always steady him. But more often than not he would fall when he was alone. Time and again my mother had to get the neighbour round from two doors away to pick him up. The next-door neighbour on the left, an arthritic old lady of 80, could hardly move herself around, let alone lift a grown man onto his feet. And the neighbours next door on the right, a young couple new to the district, didn't want to get "involved"! My brother, who once a month went up from Bognor to stay for a day or two, often put him back upright, on one occasion after lifting him out of the goldfish pond. On holiday with them one summer I came across him lying in a bed of roses. I asked him, stupidly, what he was doing there and received the laconic though humorous reply, "Waiting for you".

One escapade of his I will never forget. It happened on the last day of our annual 4-week holiday with them in London. I heard him calling and rushed outside to find him lying on the kitchen steps, blood streaming from a gash in his forehead. Coming in from the garden, he had lost his balance and hit his head on the free-standing handrail erected alongside the steps to facilitate getting in and out of the house. I picked him up, Doris cleaned and treated the injury to his head, my mother stood around wringing her hands. With the blood staunched we began to think it not so bad, but phoned the hospital, nevertheless, for someone to come and look at him. When the ambulance finally arrived – six hours later! – an X-ray was suggested to make sure no internal injury had occurred. I accompanied him to the hospital. It was well past midnight when they wheeled him into the X-ray unit and 2 o'clock in the morning when the taxi arrived back home. It was the shortest night I ever spent in bed: Doris and I were leaving for Vienna nine hours later on the 11 a.m. plane from Heathrow.

Towards the end my stepfather's life must have been, like that of many another, a martyrdom. Apart from the fact that my mother had grown very deaf and wouldn't wear her hearing aid he developed arthritis in his hands and couldn't open jars and bottles. The biggest problem for him occurred at bedtime. To make it easier for my mother to get in and out of bed he'd had a second mattress placed on top of the first. For him going to bed must have been like climbing Mount Everest. But he never complained. He took it all in his stride. He would clamber onto the bed as best he could and with a special self-devised gadget pull his legs up after him, first the left, then the right.

We were amazed that he could still drive the car. Pedal operation requires a certain amount of leg control, which we thought he had. For him motoring came to an abrupt end one day, thankfully without any loss of life. Our daughter, on holiday with them, told us about it. On leaving a petrol filling station he somehow got the pedals mixed up. He floored the accelerator instead of the brake pedal, thereby knocking down one of the petrol pumps. After which he drove the car smartly into a nearby hedge. If it had been a brick wall none of the car'sd occupants would have lived to tell the tale

A stickler for accuracy, he was a difficult person to live with in younger years, but, like us all, he mellowed with age and I grew to love him. He was devoted to my mother and hurried to fulfil her every wish. What he hadn't been able to do for his mother (she was gassed, with the rest of the family, in one of Hitler's concentration camps) he made up for by spoiling mine. It must have been most distressful for him when he grew incapable of caring for her as he saw fit. Plagued by polyarthritis, she wasn't so nimble on her feet either, and when she fell, which sometimes happened late at night in the bedroom, he took to phoning the police station for help, lowering the doorkey from the bedroom window on a piece of string to whoever came to the rescue. On one occasion no one answered the call at the local police station. So he promptly called Scotland Yard. Someone must have received a sound bollocking that night.

***

The meal at that restaurant was once more an unforgettable experience, although the amount of food Doris and I consumed was peanuts compared to what those around us were putting away. We felt sorry for John, not yet able to appreciate such delicacies, but he didn't seem be suffering unduly on that score. Most of the time he kept eyeing the beach wistfully, perhaps wishing he hadn't come with us. We declined a dessert and, having drained our glasses, paid and strolled off back, carwards, along the promenade. At the break in the railings we paused for a moment, and John glanced towards the beach, but the girl in the black swimsuit had gone Aware that not every woman is designed to appreciate John's forwardness, I later began to suspect that she had taken flight while the going was good. I felt genuinely sorry for him, but if he was disappointed that she had done a bunk, so to speak, he didn't show it. As it turned out, he had arranged to see her the next day. Added to that, his attention had been diverted by an icecream stall and he was intent on having a cone. He bought two, one for him and, at my request, only one for Doris and me to share. As a boy I ate enough icecream to last me a lifetime and can't understand why people still go so wild about it, considering the now universal struggle against adiposity. Vienna, incidentally, abounds with Italian icecream parlours, which close during the winter months. And the Viennese, young and old, can't wait, it seems, for them to re-open, for from the first day onwards you'll see them queuing for the stuff, or sitting, rain or shine, in glazed sidewalk parlours, braving the elements for the brief and dubious pleasure of a goblet full of Italian icecream.

So Doris and I shared a cone and walked with John some hundred yards or more until he suddenly thought it time to take us back to the hotel. Slowly but surely we were beginning to realise what was in that big case of his. He was working on an article for a medical journal. In addition to clothes the case contained a laptop and other paraphernalia for the job. As far as I can remember, we were so replete after our meal in Mondello that we went to bed that evening on an empty stomach, or almost, eating only some of the fruit bought in Petralia soprana the day before.

13. John goes shopping

On Wednesday, after breakfast, Doris and I spent an hour on the bed – she napping, me reading. We were already outside, enjoying the morning sunshine, when John came up to us, fully dressed, car-key in hand.

"Didn't see you in the water."

"I'm giving it a miss today. Where are you off to?"

"Mondello. There are one or two things I want to buy. You two can have a day of rest."

"That was our intention."

"Where does John want to go today?" Doris asked from her lounger. She often misses less important remarks.

"Mondello," John said.

"But we were in Mondello yesterday."

"We are not going. John wants to buy a few things to take back with him."

Doris sat up. We exchanged glances.

"What about lunch?" she asked.

"I'll have something there. You can eat at the hotel."

"We'll have to," I said. "But be careful."

"Meaning don't drive too fast?"

"You know what I mean."

"When will you be back?" Doris asked.

"Late afternoon, I'd say."

With that he left us. When he was well out of hearing I turned to Doris.

"You know what I think?"

"Yes, I was thinking the same. He's meeting that girl again. But he deserves a change after driving us around so much."

"What do we do if he loses his heart in Mondello?"

"Is that likely?" Doris asked.

She was right. John has a talent for getting to know people, mostly girls. He has been all over the world, attending conferences, giving lectures, spending holidays, and when he returns he treats us to stories of his encounters with the opposite sex and hands round photos as proof. It's not that he has to go abroad to make his conquests. On the contrary! He's just as successful at home. Doris and I have, in fact, lost count of the number of girl-friends he's had since we got to know him. But he fights shy of marriage and won't even cohabit with the opposite sex. It's a subject we rarely discuss and when we do sometimes get round to it I never offer advice one way or the other. Although I firmly believe that woman was made to live with man, or man with woman, I have seen too many unhappy matches to want to coax anyone into taking marriage vows. All I know is this and I tell him it often enough: if, when sexual appetite begins to falter and even before, either party fails to pull his/her weight, the union is doomed.

***

Like mine, some marriages do really seem to have been made in heaven, others in hell. Let me tell you about one of the latter, one in which neither party seemed to be pulling their weight. It happened more than 50 years ago. The protagonists have long since moved on to wherever it is we go when we take our leave. I was still a student at Vienna University. I needed new lodgings and found them with this couple. Not for the sake of anonymity, for they won't be worried about that any longer, but because it's a name easy to pronounce, I'll call them the Brauns (pronounced Browns). While serving in the army in Germany Herr Braun, by profession an engineer, had married a German woman who, after the war, had come to live with him in his home town, Vienna. A staunch supporter of Hitler, he had been allowed to occupy a second-floor flat once owned by a Jewish family, evicted and liquidated by the Nazis. I might have thought the miserable life he led in that flat divine retribution, had I not known of so much iniquity in the world that goes unpunished. I took two large furnished rooms overlooking the street. He and his wife lived in a smaller one at the back with one large window, from which you looked down into a courtyard – a room *without* a view. Life after the war had been hard for everyone in Austria. Many had coped, these two hadn't. They were trying to get by on his pension, which he supplemented by selling unredeemed articles bought periodically from pawnshops. By letting out his two best rooms he hoped to improve his situation. It did eventually but at a price. They were both intelligent, educated people. As an officer in the German army he must have cut an impressive figure. At home he had obviously let himself go, seldom shaving and often in pyjamas and overcoat all day. He was sixty years old, she some 20 years younger. Why had she married him? She had come to Vienna, I assumed, expecting to live in a way befitting her upbringing and, faced with this unexpected situation, instead of pulling her weight, an educated woman with an excellent command of English, she had thrown in the towel. I sometimes think I was destined to live with them to bring her back to reality. Pleased to have someone 'normal' to chat with, she would come into my room from time to time and talk about herself and her brother, who had committed suicide years before because, having experienced everything the world had to offer (how naive!), saw no point in living any longer!

One day, into the third year of my stay with them, I came home from work to learn that she had taken an overdose of sleeping pills. Her husband wanted to visit her in hospital, but she refused to see him, which was understandable, he having been the reason for her attempted suicide. He asked me to mediate and persuade her to come back to him. I went to see her several times and finally talked her into returning to him. She could go out to work, in some way or other turning her excellent knowledge of English to account. She followed my advice, qualified as a tourist guide and within months was showing holidaymakers round the city and enjoying it.

One day, some time later, Mr. Braun again asked me into their room for a chat. His wife was expecting. What did I know about it? It seemed I was a prime suspect. But she was three months pregnant, meaning, I pointed out, that it must have happened while I was abroad on holiday. Perhaps one of the many tourists she had shown around was to blame. Anyway, I had a clear conscience and nothing to worry about, except that I had to find new digs: with an addition to the family they would now need the rooms I was occupying. I met Mrs. Braun once, by chance, some years later. She had taken a new lease on life. The child was a boy, the joy of her life. She was still living with her husband. I wished to be remembered to him. Perhaps they were now happy together. I didn't ask.

I can't resist telling you about another marriage made elsewhere than in heaven. While I was lodging with the Braun family I got to know a girl – through a 'lonely hearts' ad. She was a very nice and very intelligent and we had good times together but no sex. In those days one didn't hop into bed so readily. Well, I didn't! In the carnival season she suggested going to a fancy-dress ball. I acquiesced. We went. There she fell head over heels in love with a journalist. They danced with each other, in close embrace, all evening, leaving me to my own devices. A week later she phoned me. They couldn't live apart. They were getting married. It was a rush affair. Her brother, I think, was best man, but I was invited round some days after the wedding to drink champagne with them. They wanted to thank me for bringing them together. After all, I had taken her to the ball, where she had met the love of her life. They looked so gloriously happy as we sat there sipping champagne in her flat that I felt envious. Six weeks later I received a phone call from the husband. Would I meet him in the evening? We met. He wanted me to go with him on a tour of Africa, helping him to write a travel book or something of the kind. But how could he want to leave his wife, I asked. That was exactly why he wanted to go: to get as far way from her as possible. He couldn't stand the sight of her. If he didn't do something to get her out of his system he would go mad. How often does that sort of thing happen? Is that love? At first you can't live apart; later you can't live together. Is it any wonder that I never urge John to get married and settle down?

***

It must have been about 1:30 when, after enjoying the sunshine and leafing through the books we had with us, Doris and I agreed to think about lunch somewhere. It wasn't so long after breakfast but, understandably, we hadn't exactly eaten our heads off. We had decided to try the place next door, access to which was along the shore, and were about to rise from our loungers and go indoors to change into less flimsy clothing when John came strolling towards us.
"What are you doing back so early?"
"Can't you guess?"
"She wasn't there."
"Correct."
Doris turned and saw him.
"He's back, heartbroken," I said. Then, "What have you got there?"
He was holding two large carrier bags.

111

"Things to wear."

He opened one of the bags and drew out a light–weight fawn jacket.

"Very nice," I said. "And trousers to go with it?"

"No, another jacket."

The second one he produced was of corduroy.

"Two jackets and no trousers?"

"I got them cheap."

"Pay for one take two? Let's see them on you."

He put the second one on. It was a dirty green colour.

"Very nice. I'll buy you a tie to go with it."

I was kidding him. I could count on one hand the number of times we had seen John wearing a tie.

"It's very nice but the sleeves are a bit long." Doris had joined in. "They'll need shortening."

"You could do that for him," I said. "And look at all the room in it for middle-age spread."

"There won't be any middle-age spread!"

"There will if you don't soon cut out the spaghetti and noodles. What's in the other bag?"

If it hadn't been so early in the year I might have expected it to contain a water melon or a pumpkin even, but it wasn't anything edible.

"What the dickens is that?"

"A crash-helmet to wear on my Vespa."

A year of so before John had bought himself a blue scooter, his answer to Vienna's traffic problems. Doctors sometimes need to go places quickly.

"It cost only half the price I'd pay at home."

"And how are you going to get it back to Vienna?" Doris asked. "It's too big to go in a suitcase."

"Not in his. You could get a corpse in that."

"Stop ragging him."

"You could wear it on the plane, but it'll make you sweat."

"Stop it!"

"Yes, change the subject. Have you eaten?"

"We were about to do so."

"We thought of going to the place next door," Doris added.

"I have a better idea. We'll look for a restaurant in Trabia."

When John makes up his mind to something it's useless trying to change it. Declining to pose for us in the fawn jacket, he went off to his room to stow away his new acquisitions, we to ours to get ready. We met again in the carpark five minutes later and were soon driving up the main street of Trabia.

"We're not going to find a restaurant here," I said.

By the look of the place it hadn't changed much since the Middle Ages. We turned right, climbed a hundred metres or so, then turned right and right again, which brought us back to the main street.

"That was Trabia!" John said,

"So much for your suggestion to eat here." I was jubilant. I had been reluctant to come.

As we reached the main road John slowed down.

"Ask that chap if he knows where we can eat."

I lowered my window.

"Signore .....Ristorante?... Trattoria?"

The man pointed towards the sea. We followed his directions and took the bumpy cinder track that led seawards from the main road. Within seconds we could see the roof of a building between the trees. That was it. We parked the car and walked the rest of the way. The restaurant – Il Pescatore – was open, but we were to be the only guests. From experience I knew that weakly patronised eateries are risky affairs. However, it was well past the hour when most people eat, and at 2 o'clock it meant either taking pot luck or going without food until the evening. I couldn't expect Doris or John to do that and threw in my lot with them.

The meal was better than expected. John, again strictly vegetarian in his approach, opted for spaghetti with cheese sauce or something equally uninteresting. Doris and I had fish soup, followed by a dishful of mussels in wine sauce, which, much to John's disgust. we put away with relish. We sat on a terrace by the sea, the waves lapping melodiously on the pebbles 10 ft or so below. I could easily have spat into the water, only it's not the sort of thing I do when in company. I couldn't help thinking of that chap in Turkey I once saw in a café by the sea. He had taken a table near the edge of the terrace and thrown a fishing line (no rod) into the water. While enjoying his coffee – and obviously making it last – he kept looking over the railing to make sure the bait was still on the hook. He didn't catch anything while we were there, but he seemed to be a regular guest at the cafe and adept at the job, so the money invested in coffee must have been worth it.

***

From that Turkish gentleman, who had tied the line round his leg, my thoughts went back, understandably I suppose, to a story I had been told many years before, in the 1950s, by a mechanic, who used to check and clean the typewriters at the cartographic institute where I was for a time employed. Though still relatively young, the man was quite bald, robbed of his hair, so he said, by lightning. He had been in the city when the thunderstorm broke and, caught without an umbrella, had kept close to the buildings, so as not to get wet. Apparently he had been too near a lightning conductor when the bolt went down it. He woke up in hospital with the hair burnt off his head. From the story of how he had lost his hair he went on to tell me about three friends of his who had spotted a sheat fish in a backwater of the Danube. The sheat fish, a type of catfish introduced from America, is the biggest fish to be found in European waters. These three friends of his had seen this one, an unusually large specimen, at least 40 kilos in weight, and had resolved to catch it. A fish that big can't be caught with a fishing rod. What they thought would do the trick was a length of rope with a meat hook on the end of it and as bait a dead dog or cat. They opted for the latter, caught a stray one, killed and skinned it and set off for the backwater, where the fish had frequently been sighted. How often they went down to the Danube in vain I no longer remember. All I still have in memory is what happened to one of the three. Two of the friends had gone off for lunch, leaving the third sitting on his chair with the rope in his hands waiting for the fish to bite. When they returned an hour or so later he had gone. The chair was still upright, but the man who had been sitting on it had vanished, taking the fishing line with him. For a few days the event remained the talk of the village, a mystery – where had he gone? Then someone found him, together with the fish, five miles downstream. They had both been washed up, dead, onto the river bank. One end of the rope, with the hook and the cat, was deep within the fish's stomach, the other end was tied firmly round the man's leg, In the truest sense of the word, it seems, he had been caught napping. He must have been having 40 winks with the rope around his leg when the fish took the bait. One can imagine the struggle that ensued as he was pulled into the water, desperately trying to untie the rope before he went under. With the hook so deep inside it the fish had probably bled to death. Or had it died of fatigue?

14. About trains and train journeys

I can't for the life of me remember how we spent the rest of that day. John took us back to the hotel and then went off somewhere. Perhaps he drove back to Mondello to look for that girl or to find another to while away the time with. Doris and I probably had a nap on the bed and then lounged around in the late afternoon sunshine. I can recall quite clearly how we had to keep moving the loungers as the sun slowly sank behind the hotel, until the strip of lawn lay completely in the building's shadow. That was probably the afternoon when I drifted into the wine-bar and sat down for a while in one of the sumptuous armchairs. Doris didn't know where I was and panicked, thinking I'd gone swimming and been eaten by sharks or met some similarly unpleasant end.

I can remember hearing the trains. The track was some way back from the main road but with good hearing – and mine's not too bad despite my age – you could just hear them go by every so often, plying between Palermo and Messina. The word 'trains' brings back many memories. How many times, I wonder, did I go train-spotting with my cousins? Was it in our genes? Our grandfather on the distaff side was a signalman on the L.N.E.R.

Among the less happy train-associated memories were the tiring 12-hour journeys with Doris and daughter on the Orient Express to

Ostende to board the boat for Dover. Then there was that time, one Easter, when, for some reason or other, I did the trip alone. In those days you could actually drive your car into Victoria station to wait for the boat train. That's what my step-father did and remained seated inside it. I looked for a red car; his was cream-coloured. When I finally reached Wanstead (my parents' home) by Tube – after losing my wallet in a phone-box! – and rang the bell he had already returned, as thwarted and disgruntled as I was. Guessing it was me at the door, before answering it he slowly drew back the curtains of the bay-window, looked out and tapped his forehead demonstratively. After bawling each other out for several minutes we then promised to act differently next time. He was a Czech, you remember? A b----- foreigner and a Jew to boot, but I soon forgave him. You see, I had grown to love him.

Clearer in memory because more recent, much more recent, was the journey to Amsterdam to visit my nephew and his wife. We changed trains at Munich, where we had booked a sleeper. Travellers in Germany beware! The sleeper cars that now ply between Munich and Amsterdam and maybe on other routes have to be seen, or better experienced, to be believed. For bad design, I would say, they take the biscuit. They are double-decker affairs with spiral stairs leading up or down, as the case may be, to your compartment. These you negotiate at the risk of breaking your neck. For elderly and overweight passengers definitely not the way to travel. Inside your 6x6ft cubby hole the bunk beds leave you, if of normal size, just enough room to turn round and sit down on the bottom bunk or, if still agile enough, to clamber onto the top one. For this you would normally expect a ladder to be provided. You may be lucky. We couldn't procure the use of one for love nor money – neither going nor returning. Doris, who chose to sleep on top, climbed over my back to get into bed. My climbing over hers would have been more problematic, if not impossible. Thank goodness we are both relatively slim or we'd have had no room to stand between bottom bunk and washbasin. A deplorable arrangement. For once my wife and I are firmly of the same opinion: the person(s) responsible for the design of these 'state-of-the-art' sleeping cars should have died at birth.

Our most recent railway-related misadventure was, to quote Doris, something that could only have happened to us. We were returning from Stuttgart, changing in Salzburg with eight minutes to catch our connection to Vienna. Eight minutes to catch a connection was cutting it a bit fine but, the alternative, as we thought, being the hassle of finding a hotel for the night in Salzburg, I was determined to spare no effort. If we missed our connection it wouldn't be for want of trying. A few days before we were due to leave there was talk of a railway strike in Germany. When would it be? Before, after, or on the day of our departure? The strike was finally postponed but helped little to calm my nerves. On the station platform ten minutes or so before the train was due in, Doris's cousin's husband had the hairbrain idea of taking me up the new station tower with him to enjoy "the fabulous view of the city". Did I want to see the view of the city? Of course not, however fabulous! I wanted to board the train as soon as it came in and start praying, so as to help it on its way. But because I'm the sort of chap who never likes to hurt other people's feelings I went with him. If we had been the only ones eager to see the fabulous view of Stuttgart from the top of the new tower, getting up and down it (in the lift) would have been a relatively easy undertaking, but we weren't! We had chosen to return to Vienna on a public holiday (Tag der Einheit), and all the citizens of the city seemed to have decided to spend it viewing Stuttgart from the top of the new tower! At the top at last, following my host round, so as not to miss any of the fabulous view, I resolved to try again when in a more tranquil state of mind, not ten minutes before catching a train. If pushing for a place in the lift going up had been scary, the scramble to get down again was a nightmare. Fighting for a place in the lift we both learned some strange, new words from people of both sexes. On the platform again, where Doris was beginning to get nervous, thinking I'd decided to take a later train, we were informed that ours was running 10 minutes behind time! Why I didn't give up all hope, there and then, of catching the Salzburg connection and start planning the night anew I don't know.

Naive as I am, I thought perhaps that, like planes, trains can also sometimes make up for lost time and pinned my hopes on German Rail.

Apart from being bulky, suitcases of the kind now used for air travel refuse to fit onto the luggage racks of modern trains. In addition to two holdalls I had one such gigantic black case to cope with (sprung on me by Doris a few months before). Though containing only clothes, half of which we hadn't even looked at during our stay ("One must be prepared for all kinds of weather and one may want to go to a concert or similar function"), it must have weighed about 30 kilos. I left it, reluctantly because worried to death that someone could sneak away with it, near the door ready to heave out of the carriage the moment the train stopped. The holdalls I lifted – with the help of a younger and sturdier fellow-passenger – onto the rack and sat down, bathed in sweat, on my reserved seat next to Doris.

Under normal conditions that journey through the late-autumn countryside in such a luxuriously furnished open carriage would have been most enjoyable. But these weren't normal conditions. We were sitting in a train that was ten minutes late and had that darned connection to catch in Salzburg – with only eight minutes to do it in! Neither the voice that came, distorted, through the built-in loudspeakers nor the glimpses of the scheduled departure times caught through the carriage windows at the stations on our route did much to calm me. We were making up for lost time but only very slowly. We'd have to be at the ready! There wouldn't be a minute to spare! At eight o'clock, the time of our arrival in Salzburg, the voice again came through the loudspeakers, as distorted as ever, and the train began to slow down. This must be it, I thought. It would be touch-and-go, but I was beginning to feel more confident now. If we hurried we might just make it. I had lifted down the holdalls. Doris, behind me at the carriage door, was carrying the lighter one, I the other. I would lug the big case out onto the platform, then turn to take the holdalls and help Doris down. The train was stopping. I looked back into the carriage and wondered why we were the only people getting out. The other passengers were obviously travelling farther, probably to Villach. I hadn't time to ponder that. I wrenched the carriage door open and struggled out onto the platform. It was a large station but strangely deserted. I turned to take the hold-alls.

"Is this Salzburg?" Doris asked"

"Of course it's Salzburg. You heard it over the loudspeakers."

"But no one else is getting out."

"Come on!" I said. "We've got to hurry, or we'll miss our connection."

With my help she clambered down.

"The station doesn't look a bit like Salzburg."

"Stop talking and follow me."

I had grabbed the larger of the two hold-alls and was struggling to keep the big case upright. Not only bulky, it was also unruly. It had been designed for pulling over smoothly tiled airport floors, not bumpy station platforms. The train we had left was already moving off.

"We've got out at the wrong station!" Doris said again.

I was beginning to think she was right. It was a big station with many platforms but there weren't any people in sight. But where were we if not in Salzburg? The voice in the loudspeaker had said Salzburg. Or had it?

"This way, after me," I said, heading for the steps that led down to the underground passageway through which passengers reached the station's four or five platforms. Catching up with me at the bottom of the steps, Doris spoke again.

"We're wrong. This is definitely not Salzburg. You must find out where we are!"

I now had to admit it. She was right. We'd left the train too early. It wasn't Salzburg, and I had to do something about it.

"You stay here with the luggage," I sighed. "I'll find someone to ask."

That was easier said than done. We were standing alone in this long dimly lit underground passageway. Which way should I go to find someone? I hadn't seen anyone waiting around anywhere. I chose the next flight of steps to the right and dashed up it. Emerging, I saw a snackbar some 20 yards away and ran to it.

"I want to get to Vienna," I said to the man behind the counter.

He looked at me blankly, obviously a foreigner.

"Vienna!" I said again more urgently.

I must have been quite agitated, but he somehow guessed what I wanted and pointed. I turned and saw an office with a man sitting behind the huge window. I ran towards it. He saw me coming and opened a small hatch to listen to what I had to say

."I want to get to Vienna."

"Vienna?" He was very surprised.

"Yes, Vienna. What do I do?"

"You can't get to Vienna from here. You have to go first to Salzburg."

"If this isn't Salzburg what is it?"

"This is Salzachbrücke. You're quite a way from Salzburg."

My heart sank, but he was speaking again and pointing."That train leaves for Salzburg in five minutes. If you hurry you'll catch it."

I should have thanked him. Perhaps I did. I can't remember. I was too intent on catching the train he had indicated. It was standing only a few yards away with its motor running. I raced back down the steps to Doris, almost breaking my neck as I did so. She was worried to death.

"Where on earth have you been?"

"Finding out where we are and what to do. We're not in Salzburg. We're in Salzachbrücke," I gasped. "We're a long way from Salzburg."

"I told you we were wrong. Why on earth did we get out?"

"Over the loudspeakers it sounded like Salzburg! And I was nervous! Now, let's not argue. There's a train about to leave for Salzburg and if we hurry we'll catch it. Follow me and hurry!"

Having said that, I grabbed the larger holdall in my left hand and the big black case with the wheels on in my right and started off. Mounting the steps lugging that heavy black case almost pulled my right arm out of its socket, but we made it! Inside the carriage we chose to enter sat a woman whom Fate, it seemed, had placed there to console us.

"The train from Munich," she said, "usually gets in too late for passengers to catch that connection. But don't worry. You have another train at 9:35. It's a faster train. You'll be in Vienna soon after midnight."

She was right. When we got to Salzburg and had found the right platform Doris pointed out to me some of the passengers who had shared our carriage from Stuttgart. Although they had stayed on the train, like us they had missed the connection. I was pleased about that but in no state to dwell on it. I had carted that unruly big black case and a heavy holdall down and up two flights of steps. I was all in and badly in need of a drink.

15. Doris's birthday

Thursday, May 18, 2006, was probably the quietest birthday anniversary my wife (and I) have ever spent. I remember quite clearly. We met in the early hours of that day – at home our paths often cross in the night: Doris on her way to the loo and me returning from it, or vice versa – but I refrained from congratulating her, preferring to wait and awaken her, before breakfast, as usual with a kiss. I lay awake a long time after our meeting in the night, thinking about our rapidly shrinking future and wondering at the speed with which our years together have slipped by.

At nine or thereabouts I woke Doris and spoke "Happy Birthday" into her ear. Since it was her day she had to decide how we should spend it. I reminded her that John was probably even now planning an outing somewhere to celebrate the occasion and suggested we have our plans cut and dried, so as to be able to nip his in the bud. Doris had already made her decision in the night. She wanted another quiet day resting in the hotel grounds, that is, lounging and reading. What a wonderful idea, I thought. It would give me the chance to spend a few constructive hours with the five or six books I had with me.

John joined us in the breakfast room soon after we had settled down at our table. He had been up a long time, jogging as usual, bent on keeping his weight constant, if not able to reduce it. I was afraid he might embarrass me by showing up with a bunch of flowers in his hand. To my relief he came empty-handed with the promise of a later present. He was full of good news. His mother was still stable, which meant our holiday would run a normal course to its end, for if she were to take a sudden turn for the worse or even die she only had a day and a night to do it in. Secondly, he had been in touch with Vienna; his artisan friend was doing his best to get the bathroom finished before we returned. Having told us all that, he then began to inform us how we were going to spend the day. We listened patiently, then, as he paused for breath, I made known to him our decision to stay put.

"But you spent yesterday at the hotel. Why have we rented a car if we're not going to use it?"

"You are using it – every day."

"But it's Doris's birthday!"

"Exactly, and if it's her birthday she can determine what to do with it."

He turned to Doris.

"We've come to Sicily. I've rented a car to show you two the island and all you want to do is rest."

"Not rest, relax," she replied.

"And don't forget," I put in, "we're 40 years older than you."

"Thirty."

"Thirty-four."

"Doris is only thirty years older than me."

"Whatever the difference is, it's enough to make us both want to stay put rather than race around Sicily in a car."

"We'll go somewhere tomorrow in the car."

With that Doris had consoled him. We continued to wade through our stodgy breakfast in silence.

After an hour on the bed – recovering from breakfast – Doris and I went out into the sunshine, expecting to see John in the Med again, beyond the breakwater. He wasn't in the sea at all! He was stretched out in a lounger reading. After a while he came over to where we had taken up our position outside the hotel room.

"No swimming today?"

"Not in the sea," he said. "I'm thinking of going for a swim in the pool."

At the side of the hotel, accessed via a flight of steps, was an open-air pool, which till then I had hardly taken cognizance of.

"Coming with me?"

To his surprise I condescended, and within minutes we had changed and climbed the steps. Had it been summer, the pool would have been crowded, but it was May, to be exact May 18th, and we were the only people there, except for the attendant, who kept bobbing in and out of an adjacent room. John went straight in; I tested the water with a toe. It was not over-warm, much the same temperature as the sea. In my youth I did a lot of swimming, though rarely in open-air pools. At open-air swimming-pools in England you scan the sky longingly, looking for patches of blue and the prospect of a few minutes of sunshine. In Italy it's the other way round: the sky is blue all over and you pray now and again for a cloud to appear, so you can cool off with the least exertion.

"Aren't you coming in?" John shouted from the other end of the pool.

"All in good time."

"Jump in fast."

"And have a heart attack?"

"I'm a doctor."

"I never jump in. If I come in I'll dive. The only trouble is my trunks are a bit loose. If I dive I'll have them round my ankles."

He didn't reply. He probably thought I couldn't dive and was simply kidding, not really wanting to go in. Eventually I did dive in, and as expected, my trunks slipped to my ankles. As I was retrieving them he swam over to me.

"That was very good. I didn't think you could."

"Diving is like riding a bike. Once learnt you never forget it."

"Yes, but at your age!"

I didn't reply to that. I know I'm old but don't like to be reminded of it. We didn't stay long in the pool. The water proved too cold for John even.

"If you're set on staying at the hotel, I'll go into Palermo."

"That girl again?"

"Could be."

123

There was a mulberry tree at the foot of the steps. We tasted the berries and spat them out, then walked back to where Doris was relaxing in her lounger. John wished us a restful day together and left. I went into the hotel room to dry off and change into shorts.

***

Lying on that strip of lawn, half in the sun, half out of it, I found reading the book I had chosen too demanding and laid it aside. Of late, now freed from the bondage of work, I often ask myself why I have been granted such a long and easy life and a happy marriage. Other human beings on this planet of ours are leading monstrously unhappy lives, dying worldwide of AIDS and other terrible diseases, or perishing in earthquakes, floods, droughts, massacres, bombings, car crashes, futile efforts to find asylum in Europe, and so on. And is it more than mere coincidence that I am alive now at this particular moment of time, enjoying the amenities of modern life, instead of having been born in the Middle or Dark Ages, say, or even earlier – a thousand, a million years ago, when conditions were pretty grim for everyone? Was my birth really a chance affair? In younger years I might have answered "no" to that question, naively inclined to believe that everything that exists, including my life and everyone else's, was 'thought out' beforehand by a Creator, perhaps before the Big Bang even – if there was a Big Bang. But the longer I live and the more I see of the wrangling and suffering worldwide, man exploiting man, and the mess we are making of things – destroying the basis of our own existence – the further I get from accepting that idea. And yet, as then in Sicily, where I could look out at the blue sky and the sea, at night in Vienna, before drifting into sleep, I often find myself recalling the many strange events of my life, incidents which some people less down-to-earth than me, might tend to consider more than mere coincidence. They are all worth recounting, but I won't keep you with more than two.

Sinan, one of our Turkish friends, was a waiter at a restaurant round the corner from where we live. We took an immediate liking to him and, thinking he deserved more than to spend his life waiting on other people, lent him money to start up in business. He opened first a grocer's shop in Vienna not far from The Ranch (our summer residence) and then a restaurant in Ören, his home town in Turkey. We spent two wonderful holidays with him there – in 1999 and 2000 – accompanied on our second visit by my brother. With two supermarkets nearby the shop in Vienna didn't stand a chance, but the restaurant in Ören, opened in 2001, looked like being a success, and Doris and I were overjoyed at having been the initiators. But, as often, the Gods were jealous and nipped it all in the bud: in 2003 Sinan was diagnosed with terminal lung cancer. We did what we could for him during those last weeks of his life; the hospital was within easy reach and we were often at his bedside. He told us, time and again, in how many ways he would repay us for our kindness when he got better; we were dearer to him than his own parents. We thanked him and, though we knew he hadn't a chance, as we left him for the last time told him how much we were looking forward to his recovery.

During the four or more years of our friendship we had come to rely on Sinan's help as gardener and odd-job man. Having reached an age when certain gardening jobs are difficult if not impossible to perform, we began to wonder how we would manage without him. Before getting to know Sinan we had employed a gardener, also a Turk, but only to prune our fruit trees and, through having this new friend of ours around, had completely lost touch with the man. Then, one afternoon towards the end of June, while Sinan lay dying in the nearby hospital, the bell on our garden gate rang. It was him – our former Turkish gardener Haci (Hadjee). His wife had recently joined him from Turkey, bringing their son with her. Haci had come to make me an offer: if I helped his boy learn English, and German, he would look after our garden for us. I agreed, marvelling at the opportuneness of his visit. We left for England two weeks later, the imminent loss of a dear friend mitigated, as it were, by the strange though surely unwarranted feeling that somehow the Gods had taken our situation into account. Sinan passed away while we were on holiday in Bognor, but we had a new gardener!

This second of the many coincidences of my life also concerned two Turkish friends of ours – Yilmaz and Yasha. Yilmaz, Sinan's elder brother, runs a restaurant in Vienna, where, of an evening, before or after a concert, Doris and I now often drop in for a meal. For a time, before we got to know him, he had done very well, running a bigger place on the outskirts of the city. Then, for reasons too complicated to relate, he went bankrupt and had to work, as a cook, for other restaurateurs. After Sinan's death we lost touch with Yilmaz. Then, on a chance visit to the restaurant where he was working we were surprised to learn that he was actually running it under his younger brother's name. He was paying the former tenant, for whom he had worked as cook, a hefty rent but hoped soon to have enough money to buy the place outright.

Some years earlier I had introduced Yilmaz to Yasha, a former pupil of mine, who, a qualified car mechanic, now runs his own garage. The two men had become friends; Yilmaz often had his car serviced at Yasha's garage, Yasha occasionally ate at Yilmaz's restaurant.

One evening, after a visit to the doctor's, Doris and I decided to eat out – not in the city, but at a Turkish restaurant on the outskirts near our flat. We were set on eating lahana sarmasi (rolled cabbage leaves filled with minced meat and rice) and nothing else, so that when we got there and found that there were none on the menu we were so disappointed that we decided to eat elsewhere – at another Turkish eatery further up the main street, where they do an excellent lentil soup. As we walked in I heard my name called and, turning, saw Yasha sitting there with wife and children.

"How did you know we were here?" he asked, even more surprised than we were.

"We didn't," I replied. "At the place down the road there was nothing of interest on the menu. So we've come here for a soup. What's brought you here from the other end of town? And why didn't you contact me?"

"I tried but you weren't at home."

"That's right. We weren't. We've come from the doctor's, but you know I have a mobile."

"I haven't got your number. I phoned Yilmaz for it. He hasn't got it either. But sit down and let me buy you something."

Doris and I sat down and ordered lentil soup.

"Strange, meeting you here," I said. "In fact, if they'd had what we wanted at the place down the road we'd be there now, not here."

I then enquired after Yilmaz and learnt that he was in hospital with double pneumonia. That was a surprise. We knew that Yilmaz was not enjoying the best of health. He had, in fact, been taken to hospital twice with heart trouble. On one occasion, when we visited him with Sinan in 2002, he told us he'd lain clinically dead for several minutes, his life saved by the quick reaction of a nurse, who had happened to pass the open door of his room.

At home again, after an hour or more spent over lentil soup and other Turkish fare paid for by Yasha, we fell to thinking of Yilmaz. He had been in hospital for several days, Yasha said. He was over the worst of it and well enough to receive visitors. We decided to go and see him the next day. In the corridor leading to the ward we met his assistant cook on his way out, a worried look on his face. At our friend's bedside we later learnt the reason. Yilmaz was now more ill in mind than body. He had been in hospital a fortnight and was again on the brink of financial disaster. There were bills to be paid, one of them that would tolerate no delay – from the public utility that supplied him with gas and electricity. They had given him a week to pay before turning off the energy, without which he, as a restaurateur, could not operate. We also learnt from him how he had managed to buy the tenancy. Years before, through Sinan, his brother, I had let him have money to pay off debts outstanding from his bankruptcy days. He had saved some of it and with that and what he had earned as a cook, had enough to pay the previous tenant the key-money demanded. Unable, by law, to borrow money from a bank, he was now at his wits' end. I turned to look at Doris. She nodded. We lent him the money to pay the most his bills. Within a week he was back at work and we were sitting with him at a table in what was now his restaurant. Before we left he thanked us for saving his life.

But for that remarkable chain of events by which Doris and I learnt of the predicament he was in, Yilmaz would have gone to the wall. Some people believe in guardian angels. I'm not convinced. If

Yilmaz has one watching over him, why, you might ask, didn't he (the angel) stay the bug that caused all the trouble in the first place?

***

All I can remember about the food we consumed that day at the hotel is the exorbitant price of it and the meat they put before us. Like much of the beef I have had, in my long life, the misfortune to encounter it would have been put to better use soling shoes or turned into pet food. Suffice it to say that it was probably the most disappointing midday birthday meal my wife and I have ever eaten. But Doris had wanted it that way and she bore it calmly, possibly because the effort involved in getting through the meat was being softened by what had begun to happen before our eyes. We were sitting with our backs to a parapet – over which, had we been so inclined, we could have jumped to our deaths some 20 feet below – looking towards the buffet table and thus able to survey the whole of the dining-room. We were already half-way through the main course when two couples, obviously Italian, entered and chose to sit at a table some five metres from ours and so positioned that we could observe them without turning our heads. The two women had sat down side by side with their backs to the wall. Both were very attractive and I found myself again wondering why pretty women so often opt to consort with unattractive men. The newcomers were obviously aware that we were the only other guests in the room and assuming, correctly, that Doris and I were foreigners, the men were making no attempt to speak softly. One of them had chosen to sit at the far end of the table and was most of the time thus obscured from view by his overweight companion, who had taken the chair opposite his blond partner and sat with his body turned most of the time half right, the better to converse with the other three. From time to time he would turn back to address his partner, and as he did so we saw the diamond ring flash on his ring finger. He was the heavyweight Hollywood gangster of fifty years ago and, being in Sicily, I got carried away. From the tone of his voice it was clear that his anger had been aroused by something the other had said, for he leaned towards him, his broad back straining at the seams of an immaculate grey flannel suit. I could have sworn he had grasped the other by the lapel of his jacket. Would he strangle him, I wondered, or pull a gun on him? We were, after all, in a part of the world where things like that are known to be a frequent occurrence. However, at that moment the waiter came in with their order and my gangster subsided onto his chair. I glanced at Doris. She had also been following the scene at the neighbouring table with interest and seemed as disappointed as I was to see it end so abruptly. Perhaps it was as well. As witnesses of a Sicilian murder we wouldn't have lived to tell the tale. On the other hand, we may not have been watching an altercation at all. Having such robust vocal chords, people from that and other parts of Europe, when engaged in normal conversation, often create the impression of being angry about something or other. I called the waiter and paid – through the nose, I thought, having eaten next to nothing and struggled so hard and unrewardingly with the meat. As we left the room I ventured one more glance towards the restaurant's only other guests. The blond lady was looking my way. She smiled and shrugged her shoulders. Was she apologizing for not having kept her partner under control. Or was she saying she thought me attractive but couldn't do much about it?

16. I dream the future

After the tussle with the meat both Doris and I were in need of a rest. Others might have preferred to stretch out on a lounger, resting and soaking up vitamin D, but for us the only option was bed, and thither we betook ourselves. That afternoon nap will for me always remain vivid in memory because of the strange dream I had. It was one of those glimpses of the future that I occasionally experience during sleep. I was in a large room sitting at one of many tables. Somewhere far to my left Doris was singing a chanson and opposite me at the table but slightly to my right sat a dark-haired man, clearly of Italian origin. As I looked at him he told me his name. He said he was Umberto I, King of Italy. The scene slowly dissolved and I woke up, the dream content still fresh in memory. Why I had dreamt of an Italian king I couldn't for the life of me imagine, unless it was because we were in Italy. And who was Umberto I? (I have since found out. He was king of Italy from 1878 till 1900. He died in Monza, assassinated by the anarchist Gaetano Bresci.) I was still wondering at the strangeness of the dream when Doris awoke, much refreshed, and suggested spending the rest of the afternoon on the grass outside our room. I changed into a T-shirt and shorts, picked up two of the books I had with me and went out to secure the loungers. Doris then joined me, also in beachwear, and we both settled down to read,

One of the books I intended to read, bought in England a month before but not yet looked at, was 'Beyond Coincidence' by Martin Plimmer and Brian King. I leafed through it for a few minutes, undecided whether to tackle the introductory discussion of the subject in Part 1 or leave that for a cooler moment and enjoy some of the less demanding stories in Part 2. I opted for the latter and turned to Chapter 11 'Parallel Lives'. The first story was about a mix-up concerning two American women of the same name who lived in the same county in Maryland. A strange coincidence to say the least. As I followed the story down page 234 my gaze fell upon the title of the next reported coincidence 'Umberto Deuxberto'. The story tells how Umberto I of Italy travelled to Monza (near Milan) to present awards to athletes who had taken part in a tournament. On the evening before the event he went for dinner at a restaurant run by a man called Umberto, who not only bore the same name but also strongly resembled him. The King was so impressed by this that he asked the restaurateur to join him at his table, where, talking of the past, they found that they had much more in common than just the name and appearance. Incidentally, according to the story, they both died on the same day, the restaurateur in a shooting accident, the king at the hands of the said assassin. For me the story as such was of less interest than the fact that this Umberto, King of Italy, had figured in my dream, experienced an hour or more earlier. I had shared his table. He had introduced himself to me and we had been sitting in what I then realised must have been a restaurant – a room with many tables. Had I seen myself as the restaurant owner in that dream? Possibly, but why Doris had figured in my dream, singing a chanson, is beyond me. She used to sing opera, and we often said she'd have earned more money with chansons or similar songs, but she never got round to singing them.

***

Another precognitive dream of mine occurred in the 1960s, while we were spending the summer holidays with my parents in Wanstead (London). I woke up one morning with the dream still quite clear in memory; we (several people, including Doris and my parents) had been discussing the fact that there were rats in the cellar and something would have to be done about it. That same morning the next-door neighbours invited us all in for morning coffee. While we sat drinking it our host, a Mr. Luton, began to tell us that he had discovered rats in their cellar and asked us what we could suggest to get rid of them.

I have thought long and hard about the many precognitive dreams I have had. Could it be that some non-physical part of us – the spirit – has access to the future? Our dreams would seem to be concocted from both past and future events. Discovering in them elements of past experiences is easy enough because the dream rings a bell, so to speak. On waking, we remember the event that triggered it. But in the case of a future event that gives rise to a dream we have most probably long since forgotten the dream content itself, and the fact passes unnoticed. Only when the dream is vivid enough and little time passes between dream and causative experience do we stand a chance of connecting the two.

That part of us which in sleep can access the future must also, in some way, be linked to memory. Not long ago I awoke from a dream in which I had been carried back many years to play with two boyhood friends of mine, a boy and a girl who lived some few doors away in my home town. We were in their garden with their dog Shirley, an Airdale terrier. Why on earth, I wondered, had I dreamt of them and their dog after all those years? I was soon to know. That same afternoon, in the car on the way to a restaurant, we were stopped by traffic lights. While we were waiting to turn right I took my eyes off the road for a moment. There, straight ahead of us, was a huge poster of an Airedale straining at its lead to get at a bowl of dog food. I should add that in all the years in Vienna I have never seen anyone out walking an Airedale.

***

By five o'clock the hotel had cast its shadow over the whole strip of lawn, making it too cool to stay outside. So we gathered up our books and went indoors. We were hardly inside again when a knock came at the door. I answered it. It was John.

"May I come in?"

"Of course. You're back early. What's that you've got behind your back?"

"Don't be so nosey. Wait and see."

I led him through the small antechamber.

"Happy birthday, Doris!" he said, producing a bunch of flowers from behind his back.

"But John!" Doris protested. "You bought me flowers on Sunday!"

"Only a few. These are for your birthday. From Palermo. And this is also for you."

He handed her an empty spray bottle of exquisite design,

"It's empty. I thought you'd like to choose your own perfume."

"That was very clever of you," I said. "And we thought you'd gone to Palermo to look for that girl, didn't we, Doris?"

"I saw the girl."

"Really?"

"She was with another guy. On the beach. Having fun."

"So you obviously aren't her type."

"Stop ragging him. And thank you very much, John."

"If she was on the beach with some other chap how did you spend the afternoon?"

"I went shopping again."

"More clothes?"

"A shirt and a notebook."

"A notebook?"

"A laptop."

"What will you do with an Italian laptop in Austria?"

"Use it of course."

"But the keyboard's different."

"Let that be my problem."

"Did you have a meal in Palermo?" That was Doris,

"No, only a coffee. And you?"

"We ate here at the hotel." I said

"What was it like?"

"There was a mix-up in the kitchen. They served us leather instead of meat."

"It wasn't so bad," Doris said.

"That's because you still have your own teeth. More important: there are two pretty women around. But be careful. They're not alone, and the men they're with look pretty tough."

"What's he talking about?"

"We weren't alone in the restaurant."

"We're sharing the hotel with Mafiosi."

That piqued his interest, and I piled it on a bit.

"Two couples at a neighbouring table. The men were arguing over loot. If the waiter hadn't come in when he did we'd have witnessed cold-blooded murder."

"And they're staying at the hotel?"

"They had lunch here," Doris said. "And we can't even be sure they were arguing, They were merely speaking loud. And the women aren't all that pretty."

"Perhaps we'll see them again this evening," John said hopefully.

"No, we shan't. We've decided to eat next door."

"Why next door?"

"They've got mussels in wine sauce on the menu. We watched them bring them in. Mussels fresh from the Med."

"You two are mussel mad."

"And you haven't yet discovered what's good and what's not."

Doris had picked up the flowers, intending to add them to those in the vase, bought on Sunday and still looking fresh.

"Sit down," I said "and take the weight off your legs."

We sat down on the couch, and I told him about my dream. He was impressed. He knew that sort of thing occurs but this was first-hand – from the horse's mouth, so to speak.

"We forget our dreams so quickly," I said. "So what you have to do is write them down. Keep a sort of dream diary. If you wake in the night with a dream fresh in memory jot down a few details."

"I'd never get back to sleep again. Have you ever done that?"

"I've thought about it but never got round to doing it."

From dreams we went on to talk about ghosts and apparitions. I told him of a near-personal experience. It was almost forty years ago. In May 1970 to be precise. My wife's fifteen-year-old niece, then staying with her grandmother, woke up in the early hours of the Monday following Mothering Sunday, sat up in bed and stared into the darkness. She had seen her father standing at the foot of the bed. Her grandmother, who shared the bedroom with her, was convinced she had been dreaming, until the news came later that morning from the hospital in Braunau. The girl's father had been admitted in the night and had died in the early hours of Monday morning.

John then related an even more impressive story, told to him some years before. Robert and Martin had remained close friends after attending the same school. Martin, church organist in an Upper Austrian town, had agreed to play the organ at a wedding after a fortnight's holiday in Italy, his intention being to return on the Friday, early enough for a few hours' practice, and play the wedding march on the Saturday morning. When the two weeks had passed and it had got round to Friday night without any sign of Martin's return, Robert began to worry. It was unlike his friend not to keep his word. After a restless night Robert was awakened at dawn by the sound of gravel hitting the window panes. Thank goodness! His friend was back at last! That was how Martin always announced his presence. Robert got out of bed and went to the window to acknowledge the greeting, but when he looked down to the garden path there was no one there. Then his gaze wandered to the rise some 50 yards away from the house. There, waving to him, stood Martin. Robert waved back, wondering how his friend could have got so far away in such a short time. Or had he, Robert, dozed off again before walking to the window? Too tired to think more about it, he went back to bed and was soon asleep. At eight o'clock his mother woke him with the news: Martin had died in a car crash on the motorway on the way back from Italy.

To cap John's story I felt I had to come out with another. So I told him one often related to others, not more than once to be greeted by disbelief. In the 1970s, after a number of puzzling experiences with the ouija board I took to chatting with others, including my pupils, all of them adults, about the possibility of life after death. One evening after the lesson had ended a pupil approached me with a request. He had told his mother about our end-of-lesson chats, and she, a nurse at a Vienna hospital, thought I might have an explanation for something strange that had happened once while she was on night-duty. She had been sitting alone, late, in the nurses' room when she saw a patient walk past the half-open door. It was a woman who had been bed-ridden for days and had grown so weak that she couldn't even get out of bed unassisted. The nurse stood up and went to the door of the room, thinking she had perhaps mistaken the woman for some other patient, but when she looked out into the corridor there was no one there. Now, even more puzzled, she went into the ward and up to the patient's bed. The woman lay there, dead. She had died in her sleep. It seems that nurse and patient had become close friends during the latter's long stay in hospital. If the old lady, or rather her spirit, had *really* walked past the door, I suggested to my pupil that that could have been her way of saying goodbye.

***

It was after 6 p.m. when the three of us walked westwards along the shore towards the restaurant beside the hotel. It was turning dark and some of the small fishing boats hitherto anchored in the bay were beginning to move out to sea, their engines chugging. In the old days they had brought in tuna by the ton – thus the name of the hotel – but that wasn't what those fishermen were after. The tuna now in short supply, they were out for much smaller fry – sardines, whitesides, anchovies. It's foolish of me, I know, but whenever – on telly – I see fish being hauled into a fishing-boat, thrashing their lives out one against the other in the struggle to stay alive, although so partial to fish, I can't help feeling sad. What horrific ingenuity: a planet 'blessed' with water for creatures to swim about in and prey on each other, the big eating the small, and a land animal – man – with the brains and the wherewithal to catch those creatures for food – until the seas are empty.

John eyed with disdain the two plates piled high with mussels which were placed before my wife and me on that evening in Sicily in May 2006. His contempt grew as he watched us make inroads into them, sucking, over-noisily, the wine sauce from the shells. No wonder! He was sitting, as usual, behind a plateful of spaghetti or macaroni or some such pasta, probably in cheese sauce – not John, of course, the pasta!

I can remember looking across at him more than once as he struggled through the uninteresting dish before him, but what **we** had to follow the mussels is beyond recall. It could be that, not wanting to spoil the experience with anything else, we didn't have a main dish. Then, to finish with, egged on by our friend, who was paying for it all, Doris and I shared a helping of tiramisu, and I did something I had never in my life done before. With the spoon I began to doodle on the dirty plate.

"Draw something," John said.

"Draw something?" I thought he was joking.

"With the spoon. You studied art, didn't you?"

"I was undecided whether to study it."

"Well, now's your chance."

I looked at Doris, who nodded her approval, and began to draw the outline of a face. Then added ears, nose, mouth and eyes. When I'd finished scraping the tiramisu around, John said it looked like the face of Christ, distorted with pain. He was right. It was a very medieval sort of face and, to complete it, with a few strokes of the spoon I added a crown of thorns. Why I chose to draw what I did I'll never know, having long since lost interest in the fairy stories of my childhood days. Perhaps it came from deep down in my subconscious.

"Don't spoil it."

I had been about to obliterate the 'drawing', but John had jumped up and was standing, camera in hand, about to take a snapshot of it.
"Why are you doing that?" I asked
"To remind us of Doris's birthday."
That may have been the truth. On the other hand, what he later did with the photo he may have then been contemplating as he watched me draw the face, for soon after our return to Vienna he presented me with an apron (of all things), the front of which pictured me, blown up, showing off my masterpiece, the face of Christ, "drawn" not in oil or water-colours, but in tiramisu.

***

That head and face of Christ, the man who many still believe was nailed to a cross 2,000 years ago in order to 'redeem' us, dominated western art for more than a thousand years. Way back in the Dark and Middle Ages it must have been easy to make people believe that they led such pitiful lives because they were sinful and that this man, Christ, mysteriously fathered by the Creator of the Universe, had given them eternal life in a better place by dying on a cross. Nowadays many of us – unfortunately not all – can smile at the idea, for they know that it originated in a fairy story concocted thousands of years ago in an attempt to explain man's (and woman's) existence.

The setting of the fairy tale, you will remember, is the Garden of Eden, the characters: God (the Creator), Adam, Eve and the Serpent. Created from Adam's rib to be man's helper (the story was written by a man!), Eve, though informed by Adam that by so doing she will become mortal and will then one day have to die, is coaxed into tasting the fruit from the tree of the knowledge of good and evil by the Serpent, who says she will die anyway. Having 'sinned', by tasting the fruit, Eve (the temptress) then persuades Adam to do the same. They have thus now both tasted of the fruit and realise that they are naked. To hide their nakedness, presumably from each other, for there is no one else around, they look (frantically?) for fig leaves. Then they hear the voice of God, who, strolling, ogrelike, in His garden, not yet omniscient, is not sure of the sinners' exact whereabouts and asks Adam where he is. Adam apologizes, saying he hid himself, so as not to be seen. God now knows that these two creatures of his have eaten of the forbidden fruit. Adam, male-like, blames it onto Eve, who, called to account, passes the buck to the Serpent.

Compared with the punishment meted out to Eve, the Serpent (the cause of it all) gets off relatively lightly, having merely to spend the rest of his life on his belly. (What he did before that is not said.) Eve's lot is a hard one: for her God has devised painful childbirth, (sexual) desire for man and, to cap it all, submission to his will. Adam, for not having resisted Eve's temptation must live by the sweat of his brow and, his life at an end, return to the dust out of which he was made.

For well nigh 2,000 years this curious fairy tale, on which the idea of redemption is based, seems to have been thought true throughout all the countries of Europe. For many millions of people in the world it is still part of their faith. But people of another world religion believe similarly curious things: that, for instance, a man once spoke with the archangels, who gave him a book containing God's rules for mankind, and that, later, when he died, that same man took off for Heaven from a hill, now hotly disputed, on a winged horse. Quite a number of those same people also believe that by blowing up others, so-called infidels, you can take a short cut to Paradise and, once there, invite 47 relatives and friends to join you.

Truly educated people in Europe (and America) have known for long enough who it was that hoodwinked us into thinking ourselves sinful – through inheriting 'original sin' from Adam (and Eve) – and who it was that invented the idea of a scapegoat to atone for our sinfulness. The "biggest con of all time", it held out the promise of eternal life and made many rich. Followers of that other religion have still to come to terms with their fairy tale, and the sooner the better! Before it's too late!

17. The car race in Termini

Friday dawned, promising to bring sunshine again. The promise was kept: it turned out to be the hottest day of our holiday with John. The next day and weeks would prove to be even hotter, but we were then already in cooler climes, having left Sicily to be ravaged, later in the year, by fires. At breakfast John told us of his plans for the day. For some reason or other he had to get onto the internet. Either he didn't go into detail about it or I wasn't listening carefully. A bad habit of mine. The heat was also blunting my receptivity. The sun was streaming in through the windows that stretched the full length of the breakfast hall and at 9:30 the indoor temperature was already well into the 20s (Celsius), making it difficult to think clearly. Apparently, in Mondello John had not been able to log onto the web, but not far away, to the east, in Termini he had located a possibility. He would spend the morning there and fetch us – not too early – for lunch in the same town. We agreed to his suggestion. Doris would have her after-breakfast nap and I could do some more reading. After all, why had I brought so many books with me?

***

I suppose I must have read most of the books I've collected over the last 60 years, though sometimes, when I stand and survey them in their many bookcases or open a cupboard and see them stacked there out of dust's way, I tend to doubt it. I usually know exactly where I bought them, or who gave me them, and what the cover looks like if I choose to re-read one, but what's inside most of them has long since passed from memory. I often wonder what will happen to them when I pack my bags for the last time, destination unknown. But that goes for all the possessions we surround ourselves with in the course of a lifetime and often seldom use or, after a while, even, consciously, notice.

Talking of dying, John says it's merely like going through a door into another room. If he's right, let's hope we'll all have plenty to do there to keep us occupied and happy, and that we'll see again the people we so miss in the room we, the living, are now still in.

Connected perhaps with dying are all the stories one reads nowadays about so-called near-death and out-of-body experiences. Many of them are probably invented, merely to make money. I might be inclined to take them all with a pinch of salt, it it weren't for the fact that a neighbour of ours surprised me one day with such a tale – long before the OBE phenomenon became so popularised. Her name was Beer (pronounced bear). She came in from next door way back in the early 1960s for a coffee and a chat and, seeing one of my bookcases against the wall, assumed I was learned enough to explain something that had happened to her a few years earlier. Taken to hospital with appendicitis, she'd been given the usual anaesthetic prior to the operation and suddenly found herself in a corner of the room under the ceiling, looking down on it all. The fact had puzzled her for several years, and till then none of the few people to whom she'd dared mention it had been able to offer an explanation. Having read about the phenomenon, I told her what the initiated assert, namely that she was in her astral body looking down on that part of herself which is merely physical. She listened carefully to what I had to say, but I don't think she believed me. Perhaps I didn't explain it clearly enough. Frau Beer may now be fully informed. In her late fifties then, she must have long since gone through the door John talks about.

***

Breakfast over, we went our separate ways – John to Termini, Doris to her after-breakfast nap and me to 'The Clash of Civilizations', which, stretched out full-length on the bed of our cool hotel room, I was able, for a while, to follow, with the degree of concentration and respect it deserves. Then, as happens more frequently nowadays, half-way down one of the pages I realised that I hadn't a clue what I'd been reading. I had been merely staring at the words. It was time to lay the book aside and think. It was that same troubling thought. Why had I been born into this Golden Age of European history, missing World War II and a possible death on the battlefield by a year? And why have I been granted such a long life? Why am I, at 80 years of age, in possession of all my faculties, still enjoying life, while others, half my age and younger, die of disease or are killed in accidents. And why are so many people born blind or deaf and dumb, or crippled, some so distorted as to be unable to exist without the help of others? Not far from where I live there's a school for the handicapped, and on the way to the keep-fit studio for my weekly massage I see the poor kids being wheeled around and lifted into vans waiting to take them home – to their doting parents? Some of them I see gaze skywards without seeing much, others sit there drooling, their mouths agape, heads twisted, hands distorted. What have they done to deserve such lives? And what about all those of different skin colour in distant countries mostly, starving to death, some of them barely out of the womb, of such deadly diseases as malaria, AIDS, TB, and all the rest.

Some believe the unfortunate amongst us are making amends for their bad deeds from a previous life. For most people in the West the idea of reincarnation is still regarded as wishful thinking. Asked for my opinion, I would say it's as near the truth as any of the other far-out beliefs still held, even by people considered educated.

***

When Doris awoke, refreshed by her morning nap, we went outside onto the grass and lay in the sun for a while, but not long, for reasons well enough known. Before the ozone layer grew so thin the intensity of a person's tan was often a good guide to his/her IQ. One had to be pretty dumb to want to lie around in the sun for hours on end, doing nothing. To lie around nowadays in the sun is plain stupid.

John was as good as his word. Whatever he'd had to do had been completed ahead of time, and by two o'clock we were in the car on our way to Termini. We parked in the town square, baking in the sunshine, and found a restaurant of sorts with a makeshift 'garden' outside it, protected from the sun (sensibly) by four or more huge white umbrellas. The heat had taken away all our appetites. We glanced casually at the menu. Nothing seemed interesting enough to warrant the effort of eating it. But we had to order something. We couldn't just sit there drinking mineral water. In the end, John opted for a tramezzino, Doris and I for spaghetti ai funghi. Of all the varieties of spaghetti offered by Italian restaurants, those served with mushroom sauce are my favourite, a sauce made not with field mushrooms, mind you, but with the type that grows in woods and forests, in countries that can still boast such flora. I like both kinds and have collected both – field mushrooms as big as dinner plates from the fields around Peterborough and the forest mushroom, the Boletus, as big as your fist and bigger, in the Vienna Woods.

***

Whenever I see or think about forest mushrooms, my thoughts go back to that day in 1968 when Arnold walked with us through the Vienna Woods, showing us which to pick and which to let be. And I am again reminded of the tough lot that was his to bear. Arnold would have fared better if both his parents had been Jewish. The Nazis would have rooted him out earlier, exterminated him and spared him a good deal of suffering. Born in Prague of an 'Aryan' mother and a Jewish father, he was for a long time able to evade the concentration camps, and it was not until late in the war that the SS finally caught up with him and earmarked him for Buchenwald. On the way there he escaped from the train that was taking him and other 'inferior' humans to the gas chambers and hid in the mountains until the country was 'liberated' by the Soviet army.

After the war his sister, kept in hiding thoughout it, married and went to live in a small town in the south of Czechoslovakia. As mayor of the town, her husband became involved in the country's political development, and when the communists came to power thought it better for him and his wife to leave. For years Arnold, in Prague, was penalised for his sister's defection to the West. Then came the Revolution of 1968. The frontiers were now open for Czechs to visit communist and non-aligned countries, and Arnold, with wife and son, were able to take a holiday in Croatia. While they were there the Soviets moved in to put an end to Dubcek's brand of enlightened communism. Instead of returning to a Prague occupied by a foreign power Arnold and family chose to cross the border to Austria and, because I was related to him through my Jewish stepfather, contacted me in Vienna. They stayed with us for a few days, until they were found more spacious accommodation elsewhere in the city. Arnold had worked in the paper-making industry and applied for a job in Switzerland, which he got. But his sister and brother-in-law, now long since established in the US and running a free-Czech newspaper there, insisted he should go and live with them. Much to our regret he went. Some few months later we received news of his death. He had died of a heart attack they said. Kept in the dark as to the cause of his death, we assumed he had died of a broken heart. We were right, but his heart had been broken in a different way. It wasn't until many years later that we learnt the truth – over his sister's lips. Arnold's wife had succumbed to her brother-in-law's advances. Arnold hung himself in the cellar of his sister's home.

Forest mushrooms, incidentally, fried and eaten for breakfast with a fried egg and bacon, can be the cat's whiskers, when fresh! Let them go off and they develop a smell worse than most other forms of rotting vegetation, onions included!

I ought not to have bought those mushrooms on that Saturday morning, but they were going cheap at the market and, despite Doris's warning that at the price asked they would surely not all be fresh, I couldn't resist buying them, They were on show in oblong baskets with a top layer of large recently picked specimens carefully arranged over a majority of smaller ones of less recent vintage. I knew I wasn't getting something for nothing – When does that ever happen? – but I thought that if I got them home quickly enough I could at least salvage half and, at the price charged for them, it would still be good value for money. My brother Alan, on holiday with us at the time and as keen as I am on mushrooms, was all for it. We would have those in the top layer that evening and/or the next morning fried with bacon. The rest, those cleverly hidden from sight, would come in for preparing a goulash or could be sliced and dried in the sun and kept for making soup. It was a hot day and I drove the car back to The Ranch as fast as I could but, as it turned out, not fast enough.. By the time we got the mushrooms home even those in the top layer were beginning to wilt. It was apparent that time was running out fast. Having helped unpack the other things we'd bought, Alan and I, accompanied by discouraging comments from Doris, sat down to sort

143

the mushrooms – the fresh from the not so fresh. The top layer removed, even I began to doubt the edibility of the rest, for their somewhat strange smell had started to attract house-flies and blue-bottles. Doris, who was making us all a cup of tea in the kitchen, then came out onto the terrace, where Alan and I sat working hard and asked us, exaggerating as usual, whether I intended to poison us all.

Much as we would have liked to eat those cunningly concealed mushrooms – flavoured with herbs and garlic, a few of them could have been transformed into a goulash of sorts – we decided they would have to be discarded, but how and where? The best way to get rid of them, I thought, would be to bury them in the garden. Not all in one spot. Just a little here and a little there. Unusable as food, they could make up for it as manure – ashes to ashes dust to dust sort of thing. To me, digging them into the soil seemed a sensible idea. Doris said they smelt too foul to be disposed of in that way but, then, she has a keen sense of smell, much keener than either mine or Alan's. I reckon the neighbours on both sides are similarly endowed, for they soon began to complain. The lady to the left asked me if I'd been spreading pig manure, and the elderly gentleman to the right concluded his sewer had become clogged and thought of contacting the town council to put things right. After a day or two, as the mushrooms continued to decompose, even I began to catch a whiff now and then, but by that time it was too late to do much about it. I'd forgotten where we'd buried them. We prayed for rain – in vain of course! The weather stayed hot and dry! However, the smell slowly but surely began to lose its punch, with the result that the neighbours refrained from further action. Although Doris is still convinced that those mushrooms were bad before I bought them, I still think that if we'd got them home just that little bit faster we'd have been able to eat them, instead of committing them to the soil. And, as I've said, Doris tends to exaggerate

***

While we were busy eating we became aware of a commotion of sorts behind us in the square. A number of policemen – the first I had seen since our arrival on the island – were beginning to cordon it off.

We had parked in the square and our first thought was whether we would be able to leave. What was happening? Were the police hot on the trail of the mafia at last? We finished our meal quickly and hurried out of the shade into the dazzling sunshine. We were wrong. The police activity had had nothing to do with the mafia. The barriers were there, but the police had disappeared, leaving one street open for traffic to leave by. Beyond the square towards the sea something important was happening, or so it seemed. A van had driven up and a man was bawling into a microphone. He seemed very excited about something, so, instead of driving off, we decided to investigate. To hear him better, we walked closer but, try as I might, I couldn't figure out why the man was shouting with such fervour. He wasn't singing, he was shouting. I was sure of that, although at times, I must admit, I find it difficult to distinguish the one from the other. His voice was, in fact, full of a kind of expectation. We joined the crowd of locals, of both sexes, who obviously knew what it was all about. They were waiting for something to happen, but what? The square, probably the town centre, was situated on a hill, and it seemed that something or somebody was about to come up the road leading to it from the east. If only I had spent more time on Italian, instead of frittering it away on other languages, I might have been able to decipher what the man with the microphone was getting so worked up about. He seemed to be in contact with someone who was supplying him with information, and this was agitating him so. Minutes passed. The man was shouting himself hoarse. Doris and I decided to move away from the heat and the noise by strolling under the trees that bordered the square. John, undisturbed by either, had set off, camera in hand, in an attempt to preserve the scene for anyone who might later be interested in the way we had spent the afternoon of May 19, 2006. Suddenly the crowd began to cheer. Doris and I hurried out from the shade of the trees. A racing car had come up the hill and was standing, engine purring, a few yards away, its driver enjoying the crowd's cheers. The man with the microphone was now in such a frenzy that he probably didn't himself know what he was saying. He was, without a doubt, beside himself with excitement. So were the people standing around him and the car.

Slowly we began to realise what was happening. A car race was about to begin, and the man with the microphone was a sort of commentator. He then waved his hand, and the car drove off, taking the road that sloped down the opposite side of the hill. Minutes later a second car appeared, and again the man went beserk, shouting so loudly that the windows of the houses nearby began to shake. He might have been at a football match witnessing his team score a goal, so excited had he become. After the third and fourth car had been seen off down the hill we decided it was time we also went on our way. John was quite ready to take us back to the hotel. Having watched the racing cars arrive and depart, he was, I guess, itching to get his hands on a steering-wheel again.

"Did you get what that man was shouting about?" He asked me as we started off.

"Not a word of it, but it looked as if a race was about to begin and he was letting everyone nearby know about it."

"What a strange place to start a race from."

"The Italians often do things differently," I quipped.

"I hope we don't bump into any of the racing-cars on our way." Doris put in from the back

"Don't worry," John said, "they don't allow them onto the motorway."

"But it's still a long way to the motorway."

As if in answer to that John accelerated, taking the next bend at breakneck speed.

"Steady!" I said, "Or we'll have people thinking we're one them."

He didn't respond. I continued speaking.

"I can't understand why so many of us go wild about driving. I mean, a car's okay for getting you somewhere fast, but people now seem to drive around just for the sake of it. And they can even stand for hours watching others do it."

"Why shouldn't people like driving?" John replied. "Driving makes you feel bigger than what you really are."

"But big men also like driving."

"You know what I mean. Big in the sense of important."

He glanced sideways at me. I stared back blankly. John is not very tall.

"Behind a steering-wheel you can be somebody."

Same glance from John, same stare from me.

"In a way driving is a substitute for religion. Some people still go to church, others prefer to spend Sunday mornings driving."

I let him finish his oration in praise of driving, then spoke again.

"But everyone now knows what a unique raw material oil is and how we are destroying the environment by using it to power cars and aeroplanes. And yet instead of reducing our consumption of it we organise car races and air shows and what have you simply to keep people amused."

"It's the money behind it. Don't forget that."

John would have waffled on in defence of that favourite 'sport' of his, had we not reached the sliproad. He was preparing to put on speed, which would require more of his attention.

We were back at the hotel in record time, but instead of getting out of the car John told us he intended to go back to Termini and see more of the race. That would give us two oldeys time for a rest, after which we could prepare for a last evening out, with a meal in Cefalu. He would call for us at seven o'clock or thereabouts.

On the bed, with Doris asleep beside me and the commentator's voice still in my ears, I fell to thinking about the world I was in. Some people say we have become pleasure and noise-addicted, with few around who still prefer to spend their leisure hours in quiet surroundings with a book – not necessarily a bestseller, but one that requires more thought. But if machines can now do all the work, why not let them do it. That gives us humans more time for play. And with so much time on our hands why shouldn't we devise ways to while it away? And for those for whom thinking is a chore let us organize even more car races, more football matches, more tennis and golf contests, more song and music festivals, more Disneylands and theme parks, more skating rinks, more ski tracks and trails, more river and ocean cruises, more holidays on sunny beaches, more shopping malls and megastores, and for the bed and couch-ridden more quizzes and similarly inane TV shows. We are living in the

Golden Age of European Civilisation. Let us make the most of it, for who knows how much longer it will last?

***

18. Our last big meal out

John was as good as his word. He surprised us, in fact, with his punctuality, and by 7:30 we were already in Cefalu looking for a parking space. On the way there he told us more about the afternoon race. We had witnessed not the beginning, but the end of it. The town square where we had stood and watched was the finishing post, and none of us, not even John, had been clever enough to realise it.

In Cefalu, with the car quickly parked, the question again arose as to where we should have our last big meal in Sicily. Doris and I would have been satisfied to eat at the same place as before, but John's sights were set on the older part of the town and on one restaurant in particular, where it seemed one could sit in the open air and look out over the Mediterranean.

"But why not here?" I said "We had a good meal here last time."

"You had a good meal."

"You ordered the wrong dish."

"Okay, but admit it," he said. "What these restaurants along the promenade serve is very wishy washy, adapted to the tastes of foreign tourists."

"That shouldn't worry you. All you eat is spaghetti and noodles."

"In a real Italian restaurant even they taste different. Remember that meal in Palermo."

"Shall I ever forget it?!"

"Alright then, Let's find a trattoria. That place over there." He pointed eastwards. "While we're eating real Italian food we can watch the sun go down over the Mediterranean. Isn't that a wonderful way to spend our last evening!"

"Agreed, provided we find a table."

"Don't worry. We'll find one."

Then Doris chimed in.

"If we don't stop debating the sun'll have gone down before we even get there."

We followed her advice and began to walk towards the older part of the town. She was right. It was growing dark already. The sun was setting, and the place John had in mind was some way away. We left the promenade and started off along the cobbled street that led to the restaurant John had spotted. In the old days cars had been allowed down it but now it was reserved for pedestrians only, with the result that it was teeming with tourists, already in May. We couldn't walk side by side, so I went on ahead for a while. When I turned to make sure Doris and John were not too far behind I was surprised to see they had disappeared. I walked back and found them in a souvenir shop, which also sold wines and other drinks. John was talking to the shop assistant. Doris was listening. I went in and spoke to her.

"What on earth are you doing in here? I thought John wanted to get to the restaurant before the sun went down?"

"He wants to buy a bottle of almond liqueur."

"Almond liqueur? What the devil for?"

"For his receptionist in Vienna. He has promised to take her a bottle back."

"And this is the time he chooses to buy it?!"

"Don't be so loud!"

"But he could have bought it after the meal."

"Of course he could, but he's buying it now."

In the meantime John had decided on a particular brand and was handling a 1-litre bottle. He seemed about to pay, so I said no more. Then he suddenly decided to take two and fished out some more money.

"What does he want two bottles for? He's only got one receptionist."

"Be quiet!"

"And how's he going to carry them?"

"They'll give him a carrier bag."

"I mean back to Vienna."

"Let that be his problem."

"As long as it doesn't become ours!"

Eventually the purchase was completed, and we were on our way again, me setting the pace. As we approached the restaurant where John had been so intent on watching the sun go down, from the noise emanating from it it was pretty apparent that we were in for a disappointment. I was right. The place was chock-a-block, but John had set his heart on sitting on that terrace (which overlooked the Med) and, by hook or by crook, he was going to have his way, even though, as I pointed out, gleefully, the sun had already gone down while he had been buying his almond liqueur. He marched past me and accosted a waiter, who was hurrying through, his hands and arms loaded with plates piled high with "real" Italian food.

"We'd like a table for three on the terrace."

"No room, signore. And no tables for three."

Not believing him, John marched on in a north-westerly direction and through a door onto the terrace. We followed him. The waiter had been right. More like a balcony, the terrace was hardly three yards in width with tables for two only, along each side, and an aisle down the middle for access to them. As far as the food was concerned we had obviously found the right place but had nowhere to sit. Every table in and outside the restaurant was taken.

"Forget it," I said. "Let's go somewhere else."

"No, we're staying here! I want to sit on the terrace."

"But you can see for yourself. There's nothing doing. Even if there were a table free we couldn't sit at it. They're for couples only."

"We'll take two tables. You and Doris at one and me at the other."

"But we'll then have to wait till two tables are free."

"Okay, we'll wait."

"Where? The place is full."

At that moment the same waiter came hurrying past again, plates piled high with food that made our mouths water. John turned to him.

"We'd like to wait for two tables on the terrace."

"Ma dove, signore? Where?"

"We'll stand around and wait till someone leaves."

We stood around for a few minutes, breathing in the smell of "real" Italian food. The waiter then had an idea and led us into a small room, from which one could, by standing on tiptoe, look out at the sea through a small 3ftby3ft window. There was a table in it with two chairs. We stood there, undecided what to do; after all, three people can't sit on two chairs. Then the waiter reappeared with a third chair.

"Piu tarde, signore, a fuori."

"What did he say?"

I translated. "Later, outside. When someone leaves."

John sat down at the table facing the window and placed his carrier bag with the two bottles of liqueur on the floor beside him. Doris took the chair to his right, I the one to the left. I couldn't resist pulling his leg again.

"At least you can see the Mediterranean if you stand on your toes. And the food smells damned good."

"We could have a glass of wine while we're waiting." That was one of Doris's good ideas again.

"I'm not having one," John retorted. "How can that stupid waiter put us in a place like this to wait for an empty table?"

"Two tables," I corrected him

"Let's forget about sitting on a terrace and watching the sun go down and instead enjoy the good food they're serving." I had become resigned to our fate. So had Doris.

"I am not staying here!" John then said with great emphasis.

"Well, we are!" I retorted. "Waiter, bring us the menu!"

Then John must have seen red, for he pushed back his chair angrily. "I'm leaving."

Doris tried to restrain him with "John, don't be so silly", but he was already on his way to the door

"Don't forget your almond liqueur," I shouted.

He came back and picked up the carrier bag with the two bottles in it. Then stalked off in a huff.

"See you at the car. Nine o'clock."

He didn't reply

"Go to hell," I thought.

The waiter brought the menu. It was bristling with an array of dishes, which, I am sure, would have been out of this world. But, somehow, both Doris and I had lost our appetites. To reward the waiter for his trouble we each drank a glass of wine and left.

It was a wonderful evening; May in Sicily is like June in Austria. We strolled back along the cobbled street and onto the promenade; half-expecting to bump into John, but we didn't. Perhaps he'd done

151

what I'd wished him to do and really gone there. Every twenty yards or so along the prom there were benches, placed facing the sea. We chose one within sight of the car and sat down next to an elderly couple, on holiday in Cefalu. They were from Germany, regular visitors to the town who came there most years. We hadn't been chatting long when, out of the corner of my eye, I saw John approaching – with a girl on each side. He saw us sitting there and came up to us, smiling as if nothing had happened. Before I could speak he had started introducing the pick-ups. They were local girls, both quite pretty. One was a medical student, the other a receptionist or something similar at the local hospital. They were sweet and spoke relatively good English, making frequent use of the word "okay", pronouncing it "okaahee". The sound rang for weeks in our ears. John invited them to visit him in Vienna. I noticed he hadn't got his carrier bag with him.

"Where's the liqueur?" I asked.

"In the car. I dumped it."

"Where did you eat in the end?"

"I haven't eaten. What about you?"

"We had a glass of wine each."

"Shall we look for a restaurant?"

"No, we're not really hungry. Doris thinks we should get back to the hotel and pack."

"We'll do that."

We said goodbye to his new-found friends and got into the car.

"It won't hurt us to miss a meal." Doris said. She was right, but did it have to be on our last evening in Sicily?

We got back from Cefalu around 9 o'clock, which left us plenty of time to pack before turning in for our last night at the hotel.

***

The older I get the more I detest packing, It's not only the clothes you have to think about. People my age are kept alive with the aid of pills and, if wise, vitamin supplements, not just one a day, but many. Working out how many you'll need for the holiday, with a few extra just in case your main supply goes missing, takes the best part of an hour. Then, if you're a woman, there's your appearance to consider while abroad; what cosmetics will be optimal for the change of climate (if any). I almost said climate change, but beauty preparations aren't going to prove very helpful in coping with the many problems that will surely involve.

Another thing I don't like about holidays, and I've had plenty of them, is the speed at which they go by. No sooner have I arrived at my destination than I start counting the days that remain till my departure. At the beginning of a long holiday I can find comfort in the thought that the end of it is still weeks away, but whether I go for one week or six, when the holiday is over I find myself thinking or saying to myself or others, "It doesn't seem a minute since I came" or "went", as the case my be.

While we were packing John sauntered in.

"I have a problem."

"Oh," I said, "and what is it?"

"My crash-helmet is too big for the case."

"I could have told you that when you bought it."

"Do you think it would go in your holdall?"

"You must be joking."

"You could put it in upside down and fill it with other things."

"No way! The zip's on its last legs. A crash-helmet inside the holdall would be the last straw."

"Pack it separately," Doris suggested.

"How?"

"In a plastic carrier bag with a label on it."

"What if it got damaged?"

"Crash-helmets are made to stand up to rough handling."

For some reason, as Doris said that, I had a vision of John sailing head first over the handlebars of his scooter. Not a pleasant thought, but I knew what a speedster he was, and a pothole has more than once been the downfall of better men than John.

"Perhaps you're right," he said.

"Bring it round. We'll pack it." That was Doris again. She was in a charitable mood.

153

"How are you going to carry your two bottles of almond liqueur?" I asked.

"That's a second problem."

"It's the bigger of the two."

"You can't pack them in your case. That's for sure."

My wife was right about that. John has done a lot of travelling and from the exotic countries he visits has frequently tried to bring back fragile souvenirs for Doris and me, mostly with little success. Glass and porcelain don't travel at all well, unless carefully packed and transported in one's hand-luggage. The souvenirs John has brought back – bowls, dishes, vases – weren't afforded such treatment and usually arrived home chipped or even in fragments. The thought of two 1-litre bottles of almond liqueur breaking inside John's case and leaking their contents into his clothes and new laptop – sorry, notebook – made me smile again.

"We could perhaps carry the liqueur for you," Doris suggested "in our hold-all."

"That would be great. I'll bring everything round."

Having said that, he left us.

"What a suggestion to make! Who's going to carry the holdall?" I asked, annoyed.

"You are. It won't be all that heavy."

"With two 1-litre bottles of almond liqueur in it it will! Whenever we go on holiday I dislocate my shoulders lugging heavy cases around full of clothes we never wear. This time we agreed to travel light, and I have to carry other people's luggage."

"Stop grumbling. John will handle the heavy luggage."

"Like he did when we arrived. Or have you forgotten the trek across the car-park?"

"That was *our* luggage you carried. All we're carrying for John are two bottles of almond liqueur in our small holdall, well wrapped so they won't break. Alright?"

"Alright," I said, regaining my cool – just in time, for the next moment John was back with his crash-helmet and the two bottles of almond liqueur.

"I ought to buy myself a holdall like yours, but I like to be unhampered when changing planes."

It would have been better for him if he had not been unhampered on our return journey to Vienna, but how could we know that then?

We put the helmet in a plastic carrier bag, tied the handles together with string and attached a label. Then I placed the bottles of almond liqueur in the hold-all and cushioned them all around with clothes. They weren't going to break and spoil our holdall if I could help it.

At eleven or thereabouts we had completed packing, something we had done at least a hundred times in the course of our long lives together and prepared for bed. I remember it took me quite a while to get to sleep, despite the usual sleeping pill. What had been worrying me throughout the whole of the holiday was now only hours away: the gnawing fear that we wouldn't reach the airport in time. The drive to the hotel had been so traumatic that I felt sure something would go wrong on the way back. It was a straight run to the airport and we now knew the way, but there's many a slip twixt the cup and the lip – a hold-up on the motorway, an accident, a flat tyre, etc., etc. Added to that was John's reputation for missing planes. And would handing back the car take as much time as had been required to procure it? Eventually I fell asleep and within minutes, or so it seemed, daylight was creeping into the room through the gap in the curtains, left slightly apart so as to ensure we'd be up, if not with the birds, at least in time for breakfast.

19. We leave for home

To my surprise our departure went off without the slightest hitch. Our frugal breakfast was soon over, as usual, and in no time we were at the reception desk, paying for our stay. John carried the heavy luggage, our case included, to the car and we were soon on our way to the airport, stopping only to refuel. It was Saturday with little heavy traffic on the roads, and John let it rip (as usual), averaging 150 (kph) most of the way. Our plane left about midday, and the sun was already high in the sky. I had the sea on my right and was able to give it a long parting look, wondering when we would see it again, if ever, so blue and inviting. Doris and I knew the sea well; we had spent many hours by it in England, most of them buffeted by the wind or sheltering from the rain, longing for the sun to shine. In Sicily it had been the other way round – little wind and too much sun – and now from the Messina-Palermo motorway, as we travelled westwards I was looking down on what might have been some huge sun-bathed millpond stretching away as far as the eye could see

At the airport John stopped the car where a week before – or was it only a few moments – we had waited for the bus to the carpark and I had almost lost my two fellow-travellers. Adept at the job, Doris soon found a trolley, to which, with John's help this time, we transferred the luggage – calmly because we had so much time to spare. Things were going too smoothly to last. The trolley loaded, John drove the car back to the carpark or wherever, leaving Doris and me to check the luggage in. For a moment or two the sinister shape of the crash-helmet in its white plastic carrier bag had the attendant worried, but a quick inspection soon assured her that it wasn't concealing a bomb or anything of the sort, and with that we were rid of the heavy stuff.

I always sigh with relief when, hot and perspiring, I watch the luggage disappear through the flaps, destination aeroplane, knowing that I am rid of it for a while and can move about more freely. Some people, including John, frequently get rid of their luggage for good when it disappears through the flaps. When you're heading for home you can, of course, cope more easily with the loss of luggage than when on your outward journey, but whether homeward or outward-bound, it's one of those things you prefer to happen to others. John, incidentally, lost his case – the big one (with the stones in it) – quite recently on the way to India or China or wherever and had to re-equip himself en route.

***

Losing luggage reminds me of what happened once when Doris and I flew to Turkey some years ago. It was an unpleasant experience though not quite so dramatic as John's. It was, in fact, an all's-well-that-ends-well story. In the year 2001 we were invited by our Turkish friend (the one who died, aged 32, of lung cancer) to spend a fortnight's holiday in Ören, a small town on the Aegean coast some 200 km south of where Troy once stood. My brother Alan, then nearing 80, was with us on that trip, persuaded to join us by the prospect of a quick troublefree flight with Turkish Airlines. We would leave Vienna, we said, at 1 p.m., change planes at Istanbul and by 4 p.m. be in Izmir, where our friend would be waiting with his car to take us 200 km northwards to our destination.

To give ourselves plenty of time we ordered the taxi for ten thirty and were at the airport by eleven, only to learn that our plane had been delayed and wouldn't leave for at least another hour. We were also informed that the next plane from Istanbul to Izmir would not get us there till seven in the evening. Fortunately, the chap who gave us the information had got his sums wrong. Arriving in Istanbul two hours late, we learned that the flights on that route were every half hour. We were squeezed into the next plane that came along and reached Izmir around 5 o'clock.

At Vienna airport our luggage hadn't been given the conventional through-the-flaps treatment. Instead it had been whisked away, with dozens of other cases and bags, on an immense cart. That's when I should have waxed suspicious, not standing by the carousel in Izmir, waiting for it to re-appear. All the other cases came gliding out on the conveyor to be gleefully collected by their respective owners. Only ours failed to appear. What would we do, we three, if our two cases had been flown to some other part of Turkey? After 15 minutes spent watching an empty carousel rotate I began to fear the worst. Behind me was a box-office sort of affair with a woman sitting sedately inside it. I turned to it and, through the window, began to explain what she should have already gathered. She had probably been having an afternoon nap, for she hadn't a clue what I was trying to say and in response to my gesticulations merely shrugged her shoulders. Thankfully, our friend, who had been patiently watching us from behind the all-glass exit doors, his face wreathed in smiles at seeing us again, was granted entry, in order to help us. At his behest the attendant phoned Istanbul airport, to learn that our luggage was not there. It had left Istanbul, destination unknown!

The nightmare came to an abrupt end. Half an hour had elapsed since our arrival and the carousel, which had shut down for a while, suddenly came to life again spewing out passengers' cases and bags, and – lo and behold – ours were among them. They had come with the wrong plane, or we had come with the wrong and they with the right one? We reached our destination around midnight after a journey of more than 12 hours! From Alan we never heard the last of that.

***

Returning the car to the agency John more than made up for the time lost procuring it: he was with us before I had time to wipe the sweat from my brow. We walked together through passport control – there was none of the frisking experienced nowadays at Europe's airports – and on to the airport snack bar, where John, with his usual generosity, treated us to coffee, which we drank on an open-air terrace gazing out onto the Mediterranean.

On the way back we had to change planes in Rome and were expecting a wait of two hours or more for our connection to Vienna. Whenever he has a longish wait between planes John makes a point of popping off to visit the nearest city.

"But will you have time to get to Rome and back?" I asked

"That I'll have to find out."

"I wouldn't risk it. Just think what would happen if you missed the bus back to the airport."

"I'd take a taxi."

"You could still get bogged down in a traffic jam. Rome is a busy place. Anything can happen."

"What would I do at the airport? Mooch around waiting for our connection?"

"You could always read that book by the English philosopher turned novelist."

"I've finished it."

"Then buy another. There's bound to be a bookseller's at the airport".

"I'll think about it."

With that he sauntered off, cup in hand, to another corner of the terrace, to finish his coffee alone. Perhaps he was thinking of his mother and how he would tackle the situation on his return. I couldn't blame him for not wanting to 'mooch' around and brood. He'd have plenty of time for brooding on the plane, but dashing off from an airport for an hour's amusement in a foreign town is asking for trouble. And he got it!

Our respective coffees downed, we joined forces again and marched to our gate, where boarding had already begun. The flight from Palermo to Rome takes about an hour, which gives you just enough time to drink a coffee and read a page of an English newspaper (the big ones) before they start telling you to fasten your seat-belt and prepare for landing. How John managed to find out what he told me while were waiting to get off the plane I don't know unless, as he said, he really had spoken to the pilot.

"Rome's too far for a short visit."

"I told you that."

"So I'm going to Ostia. It's not so far away. Takes about twenty minutes to get there and there's a good bus service."

"Are you going for a swim? It's on the coast. It's where the Romans used to spend their holidays."

"Is that so?"

"Yes, how did you find out about Ostia and the bus service?"

"The pilot told me....... You don't believe me?"

I ignored his question. "All I can say is *Don't get lost!*"

"I'll do my best. And you be careful with my almond liqueur."

"If I get thirsty I'll drink it!"

After leaving the plane we parted, John en route for Ostia, Doris and I destination snack-bar. We found one without much difficulty and sat down to the usual – rolls of bread crammed full of salami, lettuce, tomato, cucumber. You name it, it was there in the tramezzini. Swilled down with good coffee, it made a pleasant change from the tack we had been having for breakfast for the past week. After that, to while away the time, we drifted from one shop to another, ending up in one that sold just about everything, from dolls to perfume – and books, best-sellers again, most of them in English. I then realised that for the first time in my life I had come to Italy without buying a book. I couldn't let that happen. It was now or never. I looked for something that would continue to interest me on my return and opted for one on palaeontology: 'I Dinosauri, misteri di una scomparsa'. If it weren't for the fact that for millions of years (150?) this earth of ours was the home of such nightmarish creatures I might be persuaded to go along with the intelligent design theory, but they, I reckon, put the lid on any such wishful thinking. An Intelligent Designer can't have made such a blunder. Unless, of course, it wasn't a blunder and the Designer was merely whiling away His time, biding it even, knowing that the earth wasn't yet ready for an animal clever enough and suitably constructed to exploit the many possibilities built into it? Then again, despite – or perhaps because of – our bigger brain, we surpass the dinosaurs in brutality. We are certainly better at spilling blood than they were, which is not saying much for an Intelligent Designer's foresight.

***

By the time I had made my choice and paid for the book we had to think about making our way to the gate, where we assumed the plane would be waiting to take us on board. We had assumed wrongly. We were in for a long wait. It was somehow comforting to learn that the plane would be late leaving, for John had not yet turned up. We knew he always left things like that till the last minute, but this was cutting it very fine. Where on earth could he be? Had he decided, despite a sick mother, to spend the weekend in Ostia? Half an hour or more after the scheduled time of departure we were allowed to board the plane, in which we sat for another half hour. The reason for the delay came through the loudspeakers, first in Italian, then in English, but, as often, too distorted to be understood in either language. Were they waiting for John? I wondered. His seat, a single one by the window, on a level with ours and the only one unoccupied, was then suddenly taken possession of by a male passenger, a handsome devil on his way presumably to some film studio or cat-walk in Vienna. He had no sooner sat down than we heard the door of the plane clunk to.

They had been waiting for John and had given this fellow his seat! John had missed another plane!

On short flights the pilot can hardly make up for lost time. As a result we were three quarters of an hour or more late arriving at Vienna airport. I felt so sorry for the taxi driver waiting for us there. I would have felt even sorrier if I had known what lay ahead. Through passport control, Doris secured a trolley, which we wheeled, slowly, to our carousel, so as not to have to stand around too long and wait; we know – many don't – that the sooner you reach baggage retrieval the longer you spend there waiting. Eventually our luggage appeared – our case and large holdall, then John's big case, which, with Doris's help, I lifted from the conveyor. The only thing we now had to collect was the crash-helmet, wrapped in its plastic carrier bag. Why wasn't it with the other things? Five minutes passed, then ten, but the helmet failed to put in an appearance. Obviously it had found a new owner. We had lost something that didn't belong to us. What should I do? I sent Doris off through the exit to console the taxi-driver, if still there, and went to the Alitalia office to report the loss. There were two women behind the window. One of them it seemed, was showing the other the ropes.

"I've come to report a lost piece of luggage," I said. The trainee looked blankly at me. She hadn't yet learnt a lot German either.

"Che ha detto?"

"Ha perduto qualcosa," the older woman replied. Then *she* took over, in fluent German.

"What have you lost, sir, a suitcase?"

"No, a crash-helmet."

That puzzled her. The word wasn't yet in her vocabulary, though it probably is now.

"A crash-helmet," I repeated. "You wear it on a motorbike." To help her understand I placed an imaginary crash-helmet on my head and fastened an imaginary strap. The strap part of it confused more than helped her.

"My friend bought a crash-helmet in Sicily," I continued "and it seems to have got lost."

She wasn't yet with me, so I tried a different tack.

161

"He has a Vespa in Vienna. In Sicily he bought a – "

"Ah, a Vespa. "

That word rang a bell but she got it wrong nonetheless.

"A Vespa in a plastic bag?" she then said, puzzled.

"Not the Vespa! The crash-helmet! It's a round parcel. Like this." And I cupped my hands and described an imaginary globe.

"Aha, not very big."

"No, like a big hat"

"Un momento."

I had got through to her, for hearing that last word, she came out from behind the window, walked to where the luggage emerges and disappeared through a door, leaving me angry with John for having had the crazy idea of buying a crash-helmet in Sicily.

I wasn't angry long, for the woman quickly reappeared, shaking her head.

"So what do I do now?"

"Come with me," she said, leading me back to the window. There, through the slot, she handed me a form.

"Fill this in, sir, and sign it."

At the best of times I dislike filling in forms, and this wasn't one of them, with Doris and the taxi-driver, if still there, waiting for me in the arrivals hall. But I had no alternative. I could have said "To hell with the crash-helmet!" and walked away, but I didn't. I owed it to my friend to make an attempt, though presumably futile, to track the damned thing down. I wrote out my name and address and described the lost item as "a blue crash-helmet wrapped in a white, plastic carrier bag, with the handles tied and a label attached". I was convinced that I was wasting my time. The new owner was by now probably wearing it. I tried to imagine what John would say? He'd probably pull me over the coals a bit. I placed my signature at the bottom of the form, thanked the Italian lady and hurried out into the arrivals hall. Doris was waiting with the taxi-driver, also a woman (they're doing men's jobs everywhere nowadays, often with better results for less pay). I apologized for having made her wait so long. She smiled knowingly and began to push the trolley taxiwards. She was a hefty sort of person and versed at handling heavy luggage, but

John's case had her beaten, and it took the two of us to get it into the boot.

"What've you got in here, sir?" she asked. "Stones?"

"No, it's a dead body," I replied, then added quickly "I haven't the slightest idea. You see, it's not my case. It's my friend's, and he seems to have missed the plane."

I don't think she believed me. On leaving the plane I must have switched on my mobile, for when we were about half way home in the taxi it rang. It was John.

"Where the hell are you?" I asked

"In Rome," came the reply. "At the railway station, waiting for the train to Vienna."

"I warned you not to go to Ostia. What happened?"

"I missed the bus to the airport and couldn't get a taxi anywhere."

"So you won't be home till tomorrow morning? By the way, your crash-helmet wasn't among the luggage."

I expected him to flare up, but he took it very calmly.

"Can't be helped. Things often get lost."

"I filled in a form with my address on it."

"Don't worry," he said. "See you on Monday."

***

20. Epilogue

At 11 o'clock on Sunday, the morning after our arrival in Vienna, the doorbell rang. A messenger was at the door. He handed me the crash-helmet in its plastic carrier bag! I signed for it. Not long afterwards our phone rang. It was John calling from the station. He had arrived in Vienna. I was overjoyed to be able to inform him of the good news, but he was too weary to show much appreciation. He promised to call for his case, the crash-helmet and the two bottles of almond liqueur, which had completed the journey intact – thanks to my motherly care. As we talked, a thought came into my head. Now was the chance to tell him how right Doris and I had been to insist on taking a taxi to the airport. Though worn out by the trip to Ostia and eight hours or more in the Rome-Vienna train, he would have had to fetch his car from the airport. As it was, all he had to do – thanks to my foresight! – was to go home and hit the hay. I overcame the temptation. Our friend had been commensurately punished.

His mother was discharged from hospital soon after our return and went back to live alone in her flat, which had been converted at considerable cost. Looked after by members of her family on a rota system of John's fabrication, she became something of a burden, but not for long. In July, two months after we returned, she was admitted to hospital again, where she passed away peacefully in her sleep. Doris and I attended the funeral.

I hadn't carried the two bottles of almond liqueur unrewarded. On the Monday, when he fetched his luggage, John gave me one of them for my trouble. Knowing him, I reckon he'd had that in mind when he bought the two in Cefalu.

In retrospect, even holidays marred by misadventure tend to seem more pleasurable than they really were. Despite the initial difficulties, the occasional tiff and the fact that our six days there were spent largely eating and sleeping our sojourn in Sicily ranks high on our nice-holiday list. We often think and talk of the wonderful time we had there – thanks to John!

***

Postscript

Since writing all this I have heard more about Steve (the dentist). Fate has dealt him three more blows below the belt: his mother, now over 80, has developed dementia, his step-father, age 75, has suffered a stroke and lost the power of coherent speech, and his wife has died – unexpectedly. I wonder what Lady Luck still has lined up for him.

As for me, you will remember, I had two pairs of reading glasses. Now I have none to call my own! I sat on one pair, which somebody – maybe me – had carelessly left lying in an armchair; the other pair I seem to have irretrievably lost. I had them on some time ago at John's surgery. What happened to them after that is cloaked in mystery! Perhaps they fell out of my shirt pocket and are lying in the garden somewhere, waiting to be found.